BLUE

WATER

WOMAN

BLUE WATER WOMAN

BY

KEN FARMER

Cover by K. R. Farmer & Adriana Girolami. Thanks to the lovely Julie Griffith Fiol for being the cover model for: *Bánushah Kuukuh Náttih*...the Blue Water Woman

THE AUTHOR

Ken Farmer didn't write his first full novel until he was sixty-nine years of age. He often wonders what the hell took him so long. At age seventy-five...he's currently working on novel number sixteen.

Ken spent thirty years raising cattle and quarter horses in Texas and forty-five years as a professional actor (after a stint in the Marine Corps). Those years gave him a background for storytelling...or as he has been known to say, "I've always been a bit of a bull---t artist, so writing novels kind of came naturally once it occurred to me I could put my stories down on paper."

Ken's writing style has been likened to a combination of Louis L'Amour and Terry C. Johnston with an occasional Hitchcockian twist...now that's a mouthful.

In addition to his love for writing fiction, he likes to teach acting, voice-over and writing workshops. His favorite expression is: "Just tell the damn story."

ISBN-13: - 978-0-9971290-8-3 Paper
ISBN-10: - 0-9971290-8-5
ISBN-13: - 978-0-9971290-9-0 E
ISBN-10: - 0-9971290-9-3

Timber Creek Press
Imprint of Timber Creek Productions, LLC
312 N. Commerce St.
Gainesville, Texas 76240

ACKNOWLEDGMENT

The authors gratefully acknowledges T.C. Miller, Brad Dennison and Lt. Colonel (Retired USMCR) Clyde D. DeLoach, for their invaluable help in proofing and editing this novel.

DEDICATION

BLUE WATER WOMAN is dedicated to all fans of the historical western genre. The western still lives. Take a ride with me.

This novel is a work of fiction…except the parts that aren't. Names, characters, places and incidents are either the products of the author's imaginations or are used fictitiously and sometimes not. Any resemblance to actual persons, living or dead, business establishments, events or locales is entirely coincidental, except where they aren't.

TIMBER CREEK PRESS

CHAPTER ONE

RED RIVER BOTTOM
COOKE COUNTY, TEXAS

"Oh, God, run!" encouraged Billy.

"I can't," Rita said breathlessly as she staggered and fell on the narrow game trail that perambulated through the thick woods.

The young man came back, grabbed her arm and helped her back to her feet. "Yes, you can...Now move."

He pushed his seventeen-year old girlfriend along in front of him. Her long sandy hair waved in the slight breeze as they started running again through the dense river bottom.

Billy ran past her a short distance to clear the way through the branches and briars.

Rita tripped over an exposed root and fell again. She looked back down the trail behind her and screamed.

Her boyfriend stopped and turned. "No!"

He sprinted back around a small bend in the trail to help her.

Billy's death scream abruptly stopped…

SHERIFF'S OFFICE
GAINESVILLE, TEXAS

Brothers Burton and Dwight Haywood stood in front of Walt Durbin's desk, both nervously fidgeting with their short-billed caps.

The lanky former Texas Ranger, and newly elected Sheriff of Cooke County, held up his hands to the two young men. Burton was twenty and Dwight was seventeen.

"Now slow down, boys, slow down. One at a time…Burton, you go first."

The older brother glanced over at former Deputy US Marshal Fiona Miller sitting in a straight-backed oak chair to the right of Walt's desk and then back to Sheriff Durbin. "Uh, well, you see…me an' Dee wuz squirrel huntin' along Frog Bottom, you know?…'Tween Wolf Run Ridge an' the Red?"

He looked at his brother. "Anyways, we come upon these two bodies…"

Dee interrupted. "It was a boy an' a girl. We knowed 'em. It was Tunk Merrill and Lucy Mae Carter…They was sweet on each other…"

"I'm tellin' this, Dee. The Sheriff tol' me to do the talkin'."

"You wuz leavin' stuff out, nimrod."

"Don't you nimrod me, you jaywacker. I'll kick yer butt from here to next week."

"Like hell…"

"Hey!" Walt snapped at them. "I said one at a time…Dee, you can talk when yer brother finishes. Understand?…I'll put one or the other of you upstairs in the hoosegow." He nodded at Burton to continue.

The older Haywood glared at his younger sibling for a moment, and then back to the sheriff. "Like I wuz sayin', we come upon Tunk and Lucy Mae's bodies an' they wuz tore up somethin' fierce…"

"Only their throats…"

He snapped at Dee. "I'm gittin' to that! Shut yer pie hole." He turned back to Walt. "Their throats wuz tore completely out like a bear er somethin' got ahold of 'em…but, they wuzn't touched no where's else that we could see."

"We hunt the Red River bottom from Montague to Grayson Counties an' we ain't never seen no bear, nor even 'ny bear sign." Dee looked at his brother. "Ain't that right, Burton?"

He nodded. "Uh, huh. Seen some panther sign couple times, though."

"Heard 'em, too," added Dee. "Sound like a woman a screamin'."

"Did you touch the bodies?" asked Fiona as she squinted her steel-gray eyes at the two boys.

"Uh, uh, no way, no day…Blood wuz fresh. Didn't know but what, who…er whatever done it was still close by…We run like turpentined cats," said Burton.

Fiona tried to hide a smile at their alliteration.

"Awright, boys, that'll do…for now. Believe I got the location down good enough we kin find it…Why don't you hunt on the east side of the Ardmore road fer a while?"

"Yessir, don't have to tell us twict 'bout that. Ain't no way we're goin' back down to Frog Bottom," commented Dee.

He and Burton got to their feet, nodded at Fiona, and then at Walt before they turned and headed out the office door.

"What do you think?" He looked at the attractive, raven-haired former law officer, turned bounty hunter, after the door closed.

"They saw something that scared the pee out of them, that's for sure...I have to pick up Captain Bryan and his daughter, Ruth Ann, at the depot at eleven, and then I can go out there for you...I'm sure he'll want to go with me. We'll leave Ruthie at Faye's...Definitely don't want to take her."

"How long is his furlough?"

"Two weeks."

"If I didn't have that meetin' with the new mayor and county commissioners court..."

"That's why I suggested that I go."

"How about I deputize you, to make everything legal?"

"Against my better judgment, but, just this once. You know why I resigned my marshal's commission."

"I do, but, this is a horse of a different color."

Walt opened a desk drawer and removed a brass deputy sheriff's badge, walked around his desk and started to pin it to Fiona's bustier.

"Uh, maybe you'd better do this." He handed the badge to her. "Repeat after me..."

GAINESVILLE DEPOT

The big 4x4x2 coal-fired steam locomotive released her pressure shortly after braking to a stop at the platform. Huge clouds of steam boiled out on each side and was rapidly cleared away by the morning breeze.

White-jacket clad porters pushed the four-wheel luggage dollies across the red bricks close to the tracks as passengers disembarked.

Fiona eyed the stairs at the ends of three passenger cars, and then saw a tall dark-haired man with a nine-year-old girl holding on to his hand. They stepped down the four steel steps to the platform and glanced around.

"Jim, Ruth Ann! Over here," Fiona waved from down the platform and walked their way.

The young girl released her father's hand, waved excitedly at the tall statuesque brunette and headed toward her. Her blonde ring curls bounced as she ran.

"Fiona, Fiona!" She wrapped her arms around the woman's tiny waist and hugged her tight.

"Ruthie, it's so good to see you again." She looked down at the big blue eyes and hugged the little girl back as her father walked up carrying two large carpet bags.

"I almost didn't recognize you without your uniform."

She and Captain Bryan hugged.

"That's one of the nice things about my annual furlough…I get to wear civilian clothes for a while."

"Fiona!"

They turned toward the voice and saw Doctor Winchester Ashalatubbi stepping down from the third passenger car down the platform. The white-haired Chickasaw practitioner in the dark three-piece suit and tall, uncreased black Stetson with a Red-Tailed hawk feather in the band, waved.

"Who's that?" asked Ruth Ann.

"A very good friend," Fiona answered. "Doctor Ashalatubbi, I didn't know you were coming down."

"I had a little break and thought I'd come to Gainesville and check on Bodie...and who are these lovely people?" He set his bag and physician's black valise down.

"Jim, Ruth Ann, I want you to meet a very special person...Doctor Winchester Ashalatubbi. He also goes by his Chickasaw tribal name of *Anompoli Lawa*. It means 'He Who Talks to Many'. He's a physician as well as the tribal shaman...Doctor, this is Captain Jim Bryan of the 2nd Cavalry Brigade at Fort Sill. He's on furlough...and this is his daughter, Ruth Ann."

Winchester shook Jim's hand. "Captain." He bent over, took Ruthie's hand in his and lightly kissed her fingers. "My dear, it's a pleasure."

She blushed and curtsied to the elderly man. "Thank you, sir. It's an honor."

"And please call me Jim," her father said.

"Are you staying at Faye's?" asked Fiona.

7

"I am indeed," replied Winchester.

"I have a buggy, you're welcome to ride with us."

"Very good, I thought I was going to have to take the trolley."

"It's over this way." She led them off toward the street side of the depot.

"How's that shoulder, Fiona?" asked Ashalatubbi.

"It's still a little stiff...Finally got rid of the sling, though."

Winchester nodded. "Do plenty of stretching and range of motion exercises. It will help break down the adhesions...I'll give you some wormwood salve to rub on the scar, too."

"What are adhesions?" inquired Ruth Ann.

"Mostly scar tissue, my child, with probably a little atrophy of the muscles from nonuse...The entire shoulder has to be worked to restore full capability...Takes a little time...and effort." Winchester noted her badge. "You working for Walt now?"

"Temporarily."

"I was going to ask you about that," said Jim.

"There was a double murder up in the Red River bottom this morning. Walt has a meeting with the new mayor and the county commissioners, so I volunteered to check out the crime scene for him...It seems it's a bit unusual."

"Oh, in what way?" asked the doctor.

"The victims, a young man and woman, had their throats torn out, but no other visible signs of trauma...according to the hunters that found them...I need to go right out there." She turned to Bryan. "If you don't mind, Jim."

"No...No problem...Ruthie, do you mind staying with Miz Skeans...and maybe helping Annabel with the twins?"

She squealed. "Oh, no, daddy. I've so been looking forward to meeting Annabel and her babies."

Fiona grinned. "They're a handful."

"I should probably go out there with you after I do a quick check on Bodie. Doctor Wellman told me he was fairly covered up. I'm sure he would appreciate it if I filled out the death certificates and bring the bodies in."

"Oh, wonderful. We can't take the buggy, the woods are too thick in the bottom. We'll have to pick up some horses from Clark's Livery for you and Jim...and a couple of mules for the deceased."

"Glad I brought some trail clothes," commented Bryan.

SKEANS BOARDING HOUSE

"Maybe I could go with ya'll," Bodie suggested.

Annabel looked over at Winchester. "Doctor?"

He looked up from listening to Bodie's chest with his custom-made elk antler stethoscope and scratched the back of his neck. "Well, actually, a little activity would do you some good...as long as we don't get into a hell-bent-for-leather chase with a gang of outlaws."

"Hot dang!" Bodie got up from the green velvet couch. "Let me go get my boots and gunbelt."

"What do you need your gunbelt for, mister?" asked his wife, Annabel.

"I've decided after that run-in with Mankiller, I'm not going anywhere without it...Period. End of discussion."

"Probably not a bad idea. I feel naked without mine," said Fiona.

"I hate to miss out on an adventure, but, don't believe I'm up to traipsing through that bottom country with a cane," said Brushy Bill.

Winchester nodded. "Good thinking, there, Marshal."

Bodie headed upstairs.

In a short moment, he came back down, buckling his Colt around his trim hips.

Fiona looked at Jim, the doctor and Bodie. "Shall we go, gentlemen?"

BLUE WATER WOMAN

FROG BOTTOM

The horses, pack mules and even Fiona's mule, Spot, showed signs of nervousness as they neared the area of the crime scene. They snorted and danced with their ears erect and forward—there was white around their eyes as they focused on the dark woods up the bank from the sandbar that ran along the side of the river.

"I'd say we need to leave the stock here. All their dancing around will destroy what tracks there might be," said Fiona as she dismounted. "Let's hobble them instead of trying to tie them up to a limb or something…If they happen to spook, we don't want to be afoot."

"Good idea," said Bodie.

The three men also stepped down and hobbled the animals.

They walked deeper up into the woods to where the hunters said they found the bodies. Both were sprawled in grotesque positions on the game trail.

"Everyone, watch where you step," cautioned Fiona as she squatted down and studied the victims. Noticing their hands, she lifted one of the young man's to look at the fresh dirt on his palms and under his fingernails.

She shuddered as a vision of an Indian woman dressed in all-blue doeskins—wearing an ornate cowrie shell and lapis lazuli necklace—swam briefly before her eyes, and just as quickly disappeared.

Winchester went directly to the bodies, knelt down beside Fiona, pulled a magnifying glass from his coat pocket and examined the horrific wounds to their throats. "Sweet Jesus."

He stiffened as a brief vision of a giant golden-eyed white wolf flashed in his mind. The Shaman shook his head, and then quickly looked the couple over for additional wounds—there were none.

"Holy Mother of God...Fiona, come over here," said Bodie from the edge of the trail.

She walked over to the Texas Ranger. "What did you find?

"Only the largest wolf track I've ever seen...The animal has got to be well over two hundred pounds."

"Can't be. Even Timber Wolves don't get that big and the only wolves we have in this part of the country are Red wolves...They're not much bigger than coyotes." Fiona knelt down to study the track.

"Damn, no question, that's a wolf track. It's as big as the fossilized tracks of Dire Wolves I've seen...They went extinct over ten thousand years ago."

Winchester stepped over from the bodies to look at the tracks. "Maybe...maybe not." He glanced around at the dense woods on both sides of the trail.

"Lord, I'd hate to meet whatever made this," commented Jim.

Fiona unconsciously loosened her right-hand Peacemaker in its holster. She still wasn't comfortable drawing with her left. It had only been a little over five weeks since Cal Mankiller planted his Bowie knife in her left shoulder.

"Doc, if you want to get the bodies ready to load, I'm going to backtrack them...Jim, you and Bodie see if you can follow the wolf tracks," said Fiona.

The two men exchanged glances.

"Right. It looks like there are more than one, maybe as many as four," agreed Bodie

"I'd say two are females," added *Anompoli Lawa*.

"Watch yourself," cautioned Fiona.

"You, too," answered Jim.

The Captain and Bodie headed off in one direction—she in another up toward the ridge.

Fiona followed the tracks of the couple back along the game trail uphill, stopped and knelt down. "Running," she murmured. "A little faster than before, and then stopped again...The girl fell the first time. Her boyfriend came back and helped her to her feet."

Miller's eyes scanned the brush on both sides of the trail. She spotted a clearing through the woods ahead about thirty yards almost at the crest.

The two men followed the wolf tracks down to a small creek where they disappeared into the water. They crossed and walked up and down in both directions, studying the creek bank.

"I got nothing. You, Jim?"

"Nope."

"They either stayed in the creek or disappeared into thin air…There's somethin' spooky about this…Feel like we're bein' watched," said Bodie.

"You, too?"

"The hair on the back of my neck is standin' straight up…Let's see if we can catch up to Fiona."

"Agreed," said Captain Bryan.

They turned and headed back the way they had come.

Fiona broke into the small clearing, saw two shovels, two canteens and a set of large canvas saddlebags.

There were several freshly dug holes. One was at the side of a twenty-foot diameter, five-foot high earthen mound near an oak tree.

She opened one side of the bags and pulled out a map of the river bottom and a handwritten list of Indian artifacts.

Bodie and Jim reentered the part of the trail where Doctor Ashalatubbi was securing the bodies with a ball of heavy twine from his medical valise and the canvas tarps from the pack mules. He looked up as they came out of the woods.

"Any luck?"

Bodie shook his head. "Disappeared in the creek…" He looked around. "What was that?"

"What?" asked Jim.

"I heard something."

"So did I," added Winchester.

The three men looked around nervously.

"There!" said Bodie.

"Where?" inquired Jim.

Ashalatubbi pointed. "Thought I saw something move through the brush that way."

Hickman and Bryan looked in that direction.

"I don't see anything," said Jim.

"What do you hear?" asked the Chickasaw Shaman.

Bodie replied, "Nothin', why?"

Anompoli Lawa looked at the two younger men. "That's the problem…There's no sound at all, no birds, no insects…Nothing."

15

Hickman and the cavalry officer both drew their .45s and glanced apprehensively at the dense river bottom forest around them.

A pair of gold eyes surrounded by white fur looked out from the shadows.

Fiona studied the map and noticed that the location of the mound was marked, as well as several other sites. She opened the other side of the saddlebags.

There were a number of Indian artifacts: pottery shards, some bones, a dirt-covered skull, and an ornate necklace wrapped in a linen handkerchief. It was made of cowrie shells, obsidian beads and a polished two-inch diameter lapis lazuli stone in the center, with gold flecks and filaments running through it. It was the same necklace the blue Indian woman was wearing in her vision.

Fiona held the necklace up and saw the vision once again. A deadman's finger went down her spine.

Ten minutes later she walked back into the crime scene carrying the saddlebags and joined the three men.

"What did you find?" asked Winchester.

She set the bags down, pulled out the map and the necklace she had wrapped back in the cloth.

Ashalatubbi took the map, looked at it, and then unwrapped the necklace and held it up. "Oh, dear Jesus."

"What is it?" Bodie inquired.

The Shaman looked at each of the other three, and then around at the surrounding woods. "We're on sacred land...It once belonged to the Atakapan Tejas Indian tribe...part of the Caddos...They date back many hundreds of years in this area."

"I saw a vision when I picked up the necklace of an Indian woman...She was all blue and there were several giant white wolves with her," said Fiona.

"Blue?" questioned Jim.

She nodded. "Everything. Hair, clothes...Even her skin had a light azure hue."

Jim and Bodie looked at her, and then at each other.

"As did I, Fiona," said *Anompoli Lawa*. "What we saw was an acolyte of St. Maria de Jesus de Agreda los Azule les agua Dios le Santos...the sacred spirit of the Atakapan Tejas Indian tribes...The Atakapan Tejas were also mound builders, like their relatives, the Caddo.

"Mary of Jesus was a member of the Order of the Immaculate Conception and was widely known for the reports of her ability to bilocate between the Abby in Spain and its colonies in Texas. She was dubbed the Lady in Blue, or the Blue Nun, after the color of her order's habit...The natives called her acolyte, the Blue Water Woman."

"Bilocate?" asked Bodie.

"It was said that she never physically left Spain, but was transported by the aid of the angels to the settlements of the Indians. Her Atakapan acolyte was almost as revered as she was…The tribal Holy Shaman, if you will."

Fiona wrinkled her forehead. "How do you know all that?"

The Chickasaw Shaman cocked his head and grinned. "It's a gift…" He paused. "Like I said, this is sacred ground…and it has been violated."

Fiona frowned. "In my vision of the Blue Water Woman…she was wearing that necklace. I think they have disinterred her remains." She glanced around. "And we're being watched…I sense a presence."

"You're not the only one," said Bodie.

Several sets of gold eyes watched from the dark shadows.

"The spirit of the Blue Water Woman is disturbed. She and her Guardian Spirits are still a force to deal with," said Ashalatubbi.

"Guardian Spirits?" asked Fiona.

"Yes, they are very powerful and are able to transcend between the spirit world and our world."

"The wolves?"

Anompoli Lawa nodded. "Legend has it that the Atakapan were known to be able to shapeshift…"

"Shapeshift?" exclaimed Jim.

The old Shaman looked at him. "The ability to change shape from human, or spirit, into an animal for protection or retribution."

"Like a wolf?"

"Like a wolf, Fiona...panther, eagles, hawk, bear, other humans, or even what we Chickasaw call *Lofa*."

"*Lofa*?" asked Bodie.

"Wild, hairy men of the forest...Our brothers in the Northwest call them *Sasquatch*."

"Why are you and I seeing the visions?" Fiona asked.

"For me, I'm a Shaman and, as such, am in tune with the spirit world of the Indian. The Muskogean tribes...Choctaws, Chickasaws, Chatos, Seminoles, Yamases and the Mississippian tribes...including the Atakapan Tejas and Caddos along with the Cherokee of the North American continent are descended from the great mound builders. They ranged from Minnesota to Louisiana all along the Mississippi basin well over a thousand years ago."

"What about me? Why am I seeing them?"

"We do not choose, Fiona...we are chosen. Something in your aura, I suppose...or possibly one of your progenitors...Now, someway, we must return her remains to the burial mound and sanctify that spot once again."

"How do we do that?" asked Bodie.

"We have to wash her remains in pure, blessed water and pray to the Great Spirit, *Chi-hoo-wah*, to protect and watch over her."

"*Chi-hoo-wah*? That sounds familiar," said Fiona.

"You call him God, we call him *Chi-hoo-wah*...It was the name for our Great Spirit long before the white man ever came to these shores...Do you see the similarity with one of the names you use for your God...*Je-ho-vah* in your Hebrew Bible, the *Torah*?...Your God and our Great Spirit are the same...there is only one Lord God. No matter what name we choose to call him...and he watches over all of us."

Fiona brought her hand to her mouth. "Oh, my goodness. That is truly fascinating."

"Anybody got any water?"

"Not that easy, Bodie," said *Anompoli Lawa*.

Four sets of gold eyes in the shadows surrounded the group...

SUGAR HILL SALOON
DEXTER, TEXAS

"The kids never showed back up," said Chaney as he reached into his vest pocket for his makings.

BLUE WATER WOMAN

Hayden Chaney was one of the four rough-looking cowboys at a round table in the dimly lit and smoky saloon. He wore two Colts, low. The right hand Peacemaker was holstered in a special swivel holster of his own design. He didn't have to draw it to fire.

"What do you mean, 'never showed back up'?" asked Posey Sitterly, a short, stocky man, with a full mustache.

Chaney's eyes squinted down to near slits. "Want me to draw you a damn picture? They didn't show up at the meeting place north of Gainesville...Me and Gifford waited till purtnear three, an' nothin'." He looked at the rail-thin man to his left. "Ain't that right, Giff?"

The pock-faced man, downed the rest of his bourbon and set the glass back on the table. "Chaney's tellin' it straight, Posey." He motioned to the portly bartender. "Owen, needin' a refill, while yer a restin'."

"Bossman's gonna be pissed," said Monte Wheeler. "Ain't real high on my list to be the one to tell him."

"What in hell's he want with all that old Injun junk fer, anyways?" asked the gunfighter of the group, Chaney.

"Well, damnation, Hayden, guess he plumb fergot to consult me on that," snapped Wheeler. "What do you care, long as his money's good?"

The cold-eyed young man looked up as the bartender filled his shot glass. "Nuthin'...Jest curious, is all."

"'Member what happened to Ames, when he started askin' questions?" asked Wheeler.

Chaney shook his head. "Went back to Austin, didn't he?"

The leader of the gang looked at Hayden from under the brim of his worn and dirty slouch hat from his cavalry days for a long moment. "Did he?...An' leave all his gear in his hotel room?" Wheeler spat at a spittoon against the wall next to their table and missed. "Damn."

RED RIVER BOTTOM
COOKE COUNTY, TEXAS

"What do you mean, Doc?" asked Bodie.

"I mean, the only place I know to get truly pure water is Eureka Springs, in northern Arkansas."

"Excuse me?" questioned Captain Bryan.

"There's a bottomless spring there over one hundred feet across...It forms part of the headwaters of the White River...They say it's from melting glaciers all the way up in Canada...According to legends, our people have been visiting the great healing waters for almost two thousand years.

"The water is purified by filtering through over three thousand miles of rock until it flows out of the ground at

Eureka Springs...still ice cold. Our people camped there during *Nunna daul Tsuny*."

"What's that?" asked Bodie.

"The Trail of Tears," responded *Anompoli Lawa*.

§§§

CHAPTER TWO

RED RIVER BOTTOM
COOKE COUNTY, TEXAS

Doctor Ashalatubbi tightened the last half-hitch holding the canvas-wrapped young girl's body on one of the pack mules.

Bodie finished securing the male. "How long do they stay stiff like this, Doc?"

The elder practitioner turned to the young ranger. "One to four days...depending on conditions. Actually, the bodies won't reach full rigor mortis until sometime this evening...I put time of death at around nine this morning."

"It's a bit odd they started out so early, don't you think, Winchester?" asked Fiona.

He nodded. "I do...I do indeed. It's not like they were on a picnic...Based on the map and list you found, they were on a mission."

"And not of their own making...I noticed the list included anything that could be worn, necklaces, bracelets, headbands, belts and such," said Fiona.

"Could be they were hired by an antiquities museum in someplace like St. Louis or New York," offered Captain Bryan. "Or maybe someone in the illicit black market artifacts trade."

"Not overly valuable items, I wouldn't think," said Ashalatubbi.

"Maybe they were lookin' for gold or silver," added Bodie.

"Possible, but stone age Indians didn't look upon gold or silver as a valuable item. It was far too soft to be useful. They preferred something functional like shells...which they used for bartering...Wampum, if you will, and beautiful stones like turquoise and lapis lazuli."

"The necklace," mentioned Fiona.

"Exactly...There wasn't too much of the so-called precious metals in this part of the country...other than a little gold up in the Arbuckles and the Wichitas...The Spaniards taught the Indians that it was valuable back in the fifteenth century. They showed them items they had stolen from the Incas and Aztecs."

"Do you think the kids could have been sent looking for gold trinkets in the burial mounds by someone?" asked Bryan.

"I'm not sure that's it…When Bill and I were up in the Wichitas, we heard a story about a burro train of gold ingots headed to Mexico City that disappeared. We were told the Atakapan Tejas tribe of the Caddos was responsible."

"Who told you that?" asked Bodie.

Fiona grinned. "That's a story for another time."

"I noticed one odd thing," said Winchester.

"That was?" asked Fiona.

"There's no mention of pearls on that list."

"Come again?" said Bryan.

"Fresh water pearls…Very valuable. The Atakapan and Caddo dealt heavily and traded in them…White pearls from washboard mussels, pink pearls from white-eye mussels, and the most valuable, wine and blue pearls from buttermilk mussels."

"Where would they find these pearls, *Anompoli*?" asked Fiona.

"The most prolific site was a swampy area on the border of what is now Texas and Louisiana…It became a full-fledged lake in the massive New Madrid earthquake in 1811 and the mussels became harder to find."

"That's twice I've heard reference to that earthquake," commented Fiona.

"Whatever they were after…they apparently succeeded in angering the spirits," said Ashalatubbi.

"That's why we have to sanctify these grounds?" asked Bodie.

Winchester nodded. "I believe a trip to Arkansas is in the offing…Don't see any other choice. We have evidence firsthand what angry spirits can do."

He glanced at the bodies strapped to the mules.

The group was being intently watched by four sets of golden eyes from the darkness of the woods up the bank from the river. The eyes slowly changed to a shade of antique bronze and disappeared into the forest.

COOKE COUNTY COURTHOUSE
GAINESVILLE, TEXAS

"How many deputies have you hired so far, Sheriff?" asked the mayor.

"Well, since this is my first day, your honor, only one…and she's temporary."

"She?"

Walt looked at the silver-haired new mayor of Gainesville, Cuthbert Baldwin, and then at the four County Commissioners in the room. "Yessir, former Deputy United States Marshal F.M. Miller…There was a double murder this morning up in the river bottom and she offered to investigate for me."

"Ah, yes, of course. Heard of her…She go up there alone?" asked the corpulent Commissioner of Precinct 2, Lee Brant.

"No, sir. Texas Ranger Bodie Hickman, a visiting cavalry officer from Fort Sill and Doctor Ashalatubbi from Ardmore went with her."

"Who were the folks that were murdered?" inquired the mayor.

"According to a couple of hunters that found the bodies, it was Tunk Merrill and Lucy Mae Carter."

"Great balls of fire! The parson's daughter," exclaimed sixty-year old longtime Commissioner of Precinct 3, Alan Stogdill.

"What were those kids doin' up there that time of day anyway?" asked Oscar Hocking, Precinct 4 Commissioner.

"No idea, sir…Won't have until Deputy Miller and the others get back with the bodies…and maybe not even then."

"You will coordinate your office with City Marshal Farmer's, won't you?" asked Mayor Baldwin.

"Yes, sir. He's up and around now…Still using a cane, but doesn't look to be slowin' him much. He's a hard man to keep down…Look forward to workin' with him."

BLUE WATER WOMAN

SKEANS BOARDING HOUSE

Singing Moon and Yellow Owl of the Caddo Indian tribe watched the Victorian house from the late afternoon shadowed darkness beneath a large live oak across the street.

"Anyone know the time of the next eastbound train?" asked Winchester.

"I believe it's nine in the morning," answered Fiona.

He nodded. "We'll have to catch it to Denison, and then the KATY to Vinita…We can switch there to the St. Louis and San Francisco line that goes through Monett…We get to horseback from there the fifteen miles down to Eureka Springs."

"How is it you know the route, Doc?" asked Brushy Bill Roberts.

"I go up there at least once a year…sort of a pilgrimage, if you will…The area is very important to the history of my people…If we plan this right, we'll get there on Saturday."

"What's special about Saturday?" asked Jim.

Winchester looked at the Captain. "It's the summer solstice…but a special one."

"A special one? Aren't they all the same?" asked Bodie.

29

Ashalatubbi grinned. "Every seventy years there is a full moon on the summer solstice…and this is the year. Our Algonquin brothers to the north call it the Strawberry moon as it signals the beginning of the season to harvest the sweet red berries they grow up there…Down here, the Muskogean and the Atakapan Tejas and Caddo consider it as an extra special day for the spirits."

"Well, considering the ongoing plethora of train robberies, I suspect I'd better go with you," Fiona said.

"Count me in," added Captain Bryan.

"Shouldn't be too tough a trip for my leg…I'll go too," offered Bill. "Maybe the waters can help heal my leg faster."

Annabel looked sharply at Bodie. "Don't you even think about it, mister. I'll get after you like a redheaded stepchild."

Hickman grinned and held up both hands. "Anythin' but that', Annabeldarlin', anythin' but that…I suspect Walt could use a little help around the office anyways."

"I could at that, Bodie…Got eight fellers to interview for the four deputy jobs."

"I think I need to walk off that sumptuous supper Faye fixed…How about a stroll, Fiona?"

She got to her feet from the green settee. "I'd love to, Captain Bryan."

He held the screen door to the front porch open for her, and then followed her out and down the steps. "Which way, m'lady?"

"Well, to the right will take us downtown and the left deeper into the neighborhood..."

"I've seen much of downtown."

"Then to the left it is."

They joined hands and strolled down the tree-lined street, now showing the heavy shadows of sunset. The fresh scent of wisteria hung in the air interspersed with whiffs of honeysuckle.

"This is such a peaceful town."

Fiona chuckled. "Most of the time. Faye told me that Gainesville was a wild and woolly place back in the trail drive days...There's still a few cowboys that like to twist off occasionally...as they say."

"Really?"

"If we'd have walked through the downtown area, especially along Commerce Street, we could have counted upwards of seventy or eighty saloons and brothels...the red light district, if you will."

"Guess Walt has his work cut out for him, being sheriff and all."

"There's still a lot of rustling that goes on around here…both cattle and horses. Bass told me of a ring they broke up here last summer."

"Oh, right! They wiped out a patrol and stole one of our Gatling Guns."

"Uh, huh. The former sheriff was involved. That's why they had to hold a special election and tabbed Walt for the job…Just like any town in the southwest, it has growing pains."

"Still looks like a good place to raise a family," Jim said.

Fiona glanced over at the tall, handsome cavalry officer. "Speaking of which, I think you're doing a marvelous job with Ruthie. She just has perfect manners and loves helping Annabel with the twins…"

He laughed. "Oh, she's absolutely beside herself…I think she's going to make a wonderful mother one day…What about you? Ever think about havin' a family?"

A cloud passed over her face. "I had a miscarriage before my husband was murdered." She took a deep breath. "Haven't given it too much thought while I was chasing down Mankiller."

"I'm so sorry…Well, that's behind you now."

"What are you intimating, Mister Bryan?"

He blushed. "Oh, it's just that you're a remarkably beautiful woman and…"

It was her turn to be embarrassed and her cheeks turned a little red as she looked down at the path they were on. "'Beauty lies in the eye of the beholder', to quote Plato, Captain."

She has no idea how beautiful she is. "Well, this eye is the one that counts right now."

She nodded slightly. "I thank you, kind sir." Fiona made an effort to change the uncomfortable subject. "So, you attended the Military Academy at West Point?"

He looked at her for a moment. "I did. We lost a lot of officers in the war...some to the Confederacy and even more on the battlefield. I felt it was my duty to serve my country."

"How long have you been in the cavalry?"

"I graduated at twenty and came directly west to join the Indian campaign...and that was thirteen years ago."

"What did you study at West Point?"

"The usual subjects for the military...I was partial to history and engineering, though." He turned and looked behind them. "Goodness, we've walked about a mile."

Now it was his turn to change the subject. "Guess we should head back. I could use some after dinner coffee...You?"

Fiona studied his patrician face for a moment, finally nodded and turned around.

Back at the boarding house, they met Walt and one of Marshal Farmer's deputies coming down the steps.

"Trouble, Walt?" asked Fiona.

"Zeke here says there's a situation at the Silver Dollar and the marshal could use some help."

"Let me grab my hat and I'm with you."

"How about I come along, too?" suggested the captain.

"Probably not a good idea, Jim, you're not deputized and Fiona is. Besides, Zeke, Marshal Farmer, myself and Fiona should be able to handle most any situation."

Bryan smiled. "I would say."

"You can go in and have your coffee. I suspect we'll be back before you finish your first cup," said Fiona as she stepped inside for her hat.

She and Walt got in the buckboard Zeke had brought. He flicked the ribbons over the mare's rump.

"Come up there, Annie."

They headed down Dixon Street toward Commerce and pulled rein in front of the Silver Dollar Saloon.

"Grab your scatter gun, Zeke," said Walt.

Inside, inebriated cowhands from the Flying A and the Bar M had squared off in front of the thirty-foot bar along one side.

City Marshal Farmer leaned on his cane near the bar. Walt walked up next to him as Zeke and Fiona spread off to the opposite side of the semi-crowded tobacco smoke-filled room.

"You kin git yer tin badges outta here, Farmer. This is 'tween these thievin' Bar Ms an' us...Been a comin' fer a while," said the ramrod for the Flying A."

"That's not gonna work, Bart...I suggest you back down," said Farmer.

"Ain't happenin'." The chunky middle-aged leader of the Bar M, Arley Carter, glanced over at Fiona and chuckled. "Scrapin' the bottom of the barrel now, Marshal? Resortin' to split-tails to tote badges?"

"Yer about to overload yerself, cowboy. She's..."

"I can handle this Walt." Fiona stepped forward toward the ramrod. "Now, I'm assuming that's the whiskey talking, slick nickel, because your ass probably doesn't know any better...You've got two choices as I see it."

"An' what's that, school marm?" Arley laughed and was joined by several of his men in the levity.

"One, you and your men can leave, peaceable like...or I can shoot your left ear off...Call it a lesson learned. Which will it be?"

"Why you slut, I'll show you..." Carter made a quick reach for his Colt and never got his hand on the grip, much less cleared leather as a thunderous roar filled the room like a clap of thunder.

He backed up a step, his eyes resembled saucers as he stared at the cloud of black powder smoke curling up toward the fourteen-foot tin ceiling from the barrel of Fiona's Peacemaker.

Arley slowly reached up to the side of his face, feeling of the ragged area where the rest of his ear used to be—his hand came away bloody. He dropped to his knees and tried to stop the blood running down the side of his neck.

"God damn you! It's gone! You done shot my ear off!"

"Tried to tell you Arley…You just tangled with F.M. Miller, former Deputy United States Marshal…now workin' fer me," said Walt. "You're damn lucky to be alive."

"F.M. Miller!…I didn't know…I apologize, Ma'am," said the ramrod as he got to his feet and pulled the bandana from around his neck to hold against the bloody side of his head.

"Time and effort takes care of ignorance, but stupid is forever…Everybody makes mistakes, cowboy. The trick is not to make it a habit…and don't call me Ma'am."

"Uh, what do I call you?"

"Deputy, will do for the present…Now, I suggest you have your men take you by Doc Wellman's so he can patch you up…before you go back out to the ranch. Believe your evening of gaiety is over."

"Uh, yessum, uh...Deputy. We'll do jest that." He nodded at the others and started toward the front door. "Sorry fer any trouble."

"Oh, it wasn't any trouble...for me, but I'd think twice before ya'll come back into Gainesville with mayhem on your mind. If you've got an argument with the Flying A, I'd suggest a tournament of horseshoes beats fisticuffs or gunplay to settle it."

Arley nodded again. "Shore will, I mean we won't...aw, you know what I mean...Deputy."

Marshal Farmer looked over at Fiona and shook his head as the two groups of cowboys left. "I never even seen you draw, Fiona."

"Kind of the point, isn't it, Marshal?...Never let 'em get set. Just did what I figured my old partner, Bass Reeves would have done."

"It's amazin' how quickly fellers sober up when they hear the sound of gunfire close at hand," commented Walt as they headed to the door.

SKEANS BOARDING HOUSE

Fiona and Walt entered the front, letting the screen door slam a little.

"Uh, oh. Hope Faye didn't have a cake in the oven," she said.

"Oh, dang me...Forgot. Guess I better git ready to have my head peeled."

"I heard that Mister Durbin. And no, I didn't have anything in the oven...Lucky you," said Faye from the parlor. "But, I do have a pot of coffee on the stove...If you ask nicely I'll bring ya'll a cup."

"Pretty please? You make the best coffee around."

They hung up their hats on the hall tree and walked into the parlor to join Captain Bryan, Bill, Faye, Annabel and Ruth Ann.

"Well, you were right, Fiona." Jim held up his cup. "Just almost ready for a refill."

"I suppose I should just bring the pot."

"I assume you're talking about hot coffee, Faye," said Doctor Ashalatubbi from behind Walt and Fiona as he followed them in the front door.

"Didn't see you coming up behind us, *Anompoli Lawa*," said Fiona.

"I was on the opposite side of the street...Had to send a telegram from down at the depot. Thought I would enjoy a walk too."

"I'll bring cups along with the pot and put another on to boil," said Faye. "And I do have a fresh batch of brownies."

"Knew I smelled somethin' good," said Walt as he snapped his fingers. "Love yer brownies, too."

"I'll help," said Ruth Ann as she jumped up from the floor where she was playing jacks.

"Thank you, Ruthie…You're such a sweetheart."

"Funny, I can't get her to do that at the house," said her father.

"It's because you don't have any babies for her to help take care of…yet," commented Faye over her shoulder as she went through the dining room and into the kitchen.

There was a chorus of 'oohs' from the room and a blushing Fiona walked over and sat down on the settee.

KATY RAILROAD
CREEK NATION

The big KATY 4x4x2, puffed black smoke from her stack as she chugged across the iron bridge over the Canadian River.

"Well, we're in the Creek Nation now," said Fiona as she watched the muddy waterway pass under the train from her window. "Coming into Eufala, Belle Starr's old home town."

"So far, so good," commented Bill. "No bad guys…Thought we might pick up some when we slowed down to go through the Shawnee Hills."

"Got a ways to go, yet," said Winchester.

"Are we scheduled to stop?" asked Bill.

Doctor Ashalatubbi glanced at the wooded countryside rolling by. "Not normally…Usually she just slows down enough to drop off and pick up the mail."

As if on cue, the train reduced speed through the station allowing the express car agent to throw the canvas pouches to the platform. He grabbed an identical type bag from the big iron hook, slung it inside and pulled the car door closed.

The locomotive started picking up speed as they headed toward the North Canadian River bridge.

"I think I need to make a trip to the ladies privy, now that we've pulled out of the station." Fiona got to her feet and moved along the aisleway, to the forward end of the car.

The men's privy was at the opposite end. It was considered good manners for passengers to refrain from using the facilities while the train was in a station—for obvious reasons.

She entered the tiny room and latched the door behind her.

Two men in dark broadcloth suits came into the car at the forward end while two others in similar attire entered from the back. All four wore red bandanas over the lower half of their faces. One man at each end of the car carried a sawed-off twelve gauge shotgun. The second man at the back had the money pouch from the express car under his left arm.

The leading man at the front spoke up and addressed the passengers in the half-filled car, "Alright folks, jest in case you ain't figured it out, this here's a holdup."

Winchester held the canvas bag carrying the Indian artifacts tightly to his chest and whispered to Bill, "What do we do?"

Roberts shook his head. "Those shotguns can hurt a bunch of folks."

"Git yer valuables an' put 'em in these flour sacks we're a passin' down...We want it all...Now, don't do 'nything stupid, like tryin' to hold out on us or reach fer 'ny guns an' nobody'll git hurt...These here scatterguns will cut a body in two."

Bill noticed the small privy door behind the two men at the front open and Fiona peeked out at the car. The noise of the wheels clacking on the steel rails prohibited the robbers from hearing the latch click.

Roberts glanced up at Captain Bryan seated across from Doctor Ashalatubbi and him in the opposite facing seats and made eye contact. He reached his toe out and bumped the cavalry officer's boot—the man gave a very slight nod.

Fiona stepped out into the aisleway. "Hey, peckerwood!" she said loud enough for the two outlaws to hear.

They both turned around. Guns roared. The man with the shotgun took her first round between his eyes, between his

41

brow and the brim of his dark green bowler. Almost a half-second later, the second man received a shot from her left hand .38-40 in the middle of his chest. Both men dropped to the floor like shot doves.

At the other end of the car, Bill put a .41 caliber ball from the Thunderer he carried in a shoulder holster in the back of the man's head with the shotgun.

The captain swung his Army Colt against forehead of the other. Those two also fell to the aisleway like rotten apples out of the tree.

The women passengers screamed.

Acrid smoke from the three black powder shots filled the enclosed car. Some of the men waved the noxious fumes from their faces while others opened side windows.

Fiona replaced the spent rounds in her two Peacemakers and flipped them back into her cross-draw holsters. She rotated and stretched her left shoulder and stepped over the bodies in the floor.

The blue uniformed conductor opened the door at the end of the car and staggered in. He was holding a blood-soaked white handkerchief against the side of his head, trying to stop the bleeding from his scalp. "Is anyone in here hurt? They kilt the express agent."

"Just them," Winchester said as he set the bag of artifacts on the seat and got to his feet. "I'm a doctor, let me take a look at that laceration…Here, sit down." He pointed to the seat he had just vacated, reached into the overhead bin and got his medical valise.

The surviving robber moaned and tried to sit up. Bryan stepped on the back of his neck, holding him down.

"Should I whack him again?"

"Not unless you just want to…I'll put the shackles on him…Why didn't you just shoot him?" Bill pulled out the cuffs from the back of his pants.

The captain grinned and replied softly, "Was afraid my .45 round would go through him and into the opposite side of the car…There's a woman and her little girl sitting there." He nodded at the passenger hugging her still frightened daughter. "Couldn't take the chance."

"I understand and concur."

Doctor Ashalatubbi pulled out a straight razor from his bag, unfolded it and shaved the gray hair from around the gash. He had already stopped the bleeding with some powered alum.

"Now, this is going to hurt some."

"Been stitched on before, Doc…Get after it." The conductor took a deep breath, set his jaw and closed his eyes.

Winchester threaded his curved suture needle with black linen thread and made his first stitch. A low groan emitted from the conductor's throat.

He looked the man in the face. "You all right?"

The conductor nodded as sweat popped out from his brow.

"It's going to take five...One down." He expertly slipped the needle under the skin, pulled it through and tied another knot with his forceps.

Fiona snipped the threads with his surgical scissors.

"What's your name?" Winchester asked the sixty-year old man, to distract him as much as anything.

"Miles, Miles Beck, Doc."

Ashalatubbi made another stitch. "How long you been with the MKT?"

He grunted again. "Since she first crossed the Red, Christmas Day, eighteen and seventy-two."

Winchester made the final stitch and Fiona snipped it.

"Thank you, my dear."

She nodded and smiled at the relieved conductor as Ashalatubbi wiped the stitches with iodine, and then put a thin coating of turpentine and tallow on the wound.

"Gonna wrap it, Doc?" Miles asked.

"I'll put a little wrapping of gauze around your head so you can wear your conductor's hat...Going to be a mite sore for a while, though."

He grinned. "I'll wear it cocked on the side for a while."

"That'll work…Now I have to stitch up this ne'er-do-well, here…You want to get him up in the seat so I can work on him, Captain?"

"Yes, sir."

The cavalry officer picked the smaller man up by the arm and sat him in the brown leather bench seat—none too gently. He placed the man's fedora in his lap.

Winchester examined the wound. "Believe this one is going to take seven stitches…nice work, Captain Bryan."

The outlaw glanced over at Fiona. "Beggin' yer pardon, Ma'am, but just who are you? I ain't never seen nobody could shoot like you."

Bill didn't wait for her to answer. "I love doin' this…You can tell your cell mates you're going to have in Fort Smith that you fellows ran afoul of none other than F.M. Miller and I'd refrain from calling her Ma'am…She could still shoot you."

"Oh, God…F.M. Miller…It figures," he mumbled and looked up at the ceiling of the passenger car as Winchester made the first stitch in his forehead. "Ow!"

After the robber had been tended to, Jim turned to Fiona. "I'm amazed you were able to draw and shoot the guy with the shotgun…"

Bill interrupted again, "Captain, she's explained that to me. It's called eye to hand coordination…"

Winchester jumped into the conversation, "He means that she knew when she was going to draw and the malefactor didn't…A simple matter of neurophysiology."

"Excuse me?" said the cavalry officer.

"It largely has to do with confidence…I'll demonstrate it to you when it's a little more convenient." She smiled demurely. "I did have to shoot the shotgun holder first and make it a head shot to eliminate the possibility of a spasm discharge…I was a tad slow with the left because of the knife scar."

"That will eventually go away, my child. Are you using that wormwood salve I gave you?"

"Two or three times a day…and thank you, Doctor Ashalatubbi. It is working…Patience is just not one of my long suits."

A shrill scream penetrated the interior of the railcar through the open windows. Many of the passengers jumped, and then peered outside.

"What was that?" asked the conductor.

"The hunting cry of an eagle," said *Anompoli Lawa*.

§§§

CHAPTER THREE

MONETT, MISSOURI
RAILROAD DEPOT

It was middle of the afternoon when Doctor Ashalatubbi, Fiona, Bill, and Captain Bryan unloaded their mounts down the cleated ramp from the livestock car. The horses seemed a little antsy after the long train ride, but Fiona's palomino and white painted Tobiano John mule, Spot, was calm, taking it all in stride.

"You're not going to replace Diablo, I see," said Bill as he tightened up Tippy's cinch.

"I could never replace him…he was special. But, I've grown attached to Spot. Not only is he smooth to ride with his natural amble single foot, but, he's extraordinarily smart...You remember how he helped me out against those rustlers, the Zellon brothers, up in Kansas?"

"Oh, I do indeed and I can't say as if I blame you. He saved my hide too when he pulled Tippy, me and the pack horse out of that flash flood in the Wichitas right before we met old Pike," said Bill.

Captain Bryan glanced over from cinching up his own horse. "Pike? Isn't that the apparition ya'll ran into in the cave?"

"He was," Fiona replied.

"Apparition?" asked Winchester.

Fiona and Bill exchanged glances.

"We met an old buckskin clad prospector..."

"And his jenny, Lulabelle," Bill interrupted Fiona.

"...and his jenny, Lulabelle...in the Wichitas. Come to find out later he'd been dead since 1846...fifty years ago."

"Ah, it's becoming clear now...Please continue," said *Anompoli Lawa*.

"Well, he led us to the renegades we were after, but on the way, he told us about the gold mining operation the Spaniards had conducted in the Wichita Mountains using the Tawehash and Wichita Indians as slaves...He's the one that told us about the burro train of gold ingots enroute to Mexico that went missing in Texas, that I mentioned."

"Another piece of the puzzle, I think," said Winchester as he stepped up into his saddle.

BLUE WATER WOMAN

"What do you mean, *Anompoli Lawa*?" asked Fiona.

"I believe it will all become clear when we get to the spring, my child."

ROARING RIVER

Winchester looked up, and then to the lengthening shadows of the trees from the west. "I'd say let's camp here at Roaring River for the night. It would be well after sundown before we could get to the Blue Pool."

"Blue Pool?" asked Captain Bryan.

"That's actually the name given to the spring we're going to," said Winchester.

"Blue seems to be the predominate color in our venture...Blue Water Woman, the blue lapis lazuli necklace, blue pearls, the Blue Spring...Wonder what else is next?" commented Fiona.

"We'll find out soon enough." Doctor Ashalatubbi smiled.

Bill looked at the crystal clear flowing stream. "Why is it called Roaring River?"

"We're almost in the middle of the summer dry period. What you see now is straight out of the ground. In the spring and fall the rains add substantially to it and create some raging whitewater rapids...That's one of the other reasons I come at the summer solstice...the river is easy to ford."

"Makes sense to me," Bill commented as he pulled his cane from the rifle boot where he carried it next to his '76 Winchester and dismounted.

The party looked up as two bald eagles, flying wingtip-to-wingtip, soared high overhead riding thermals, voicing their shrill cries.

"Think those are the same eagles that flew over the train?" Fiona asked Winchester.

His face lit up in an enigmatic smile. "Wouldn't be surprised." He watched as the eagles disappeared over the tree line. "I'll start the coffee and supper if the rest of you will take care of the horses and gather deadfall and driftwood for the fire.

COOKE COUNTY, TEXAS
BAR M RANCH

Three mounted cowboys stood quietly in the deepening shadows of a copse of juniper trees near the top of a hill. The sun had set over an hour earlier.

"Twilight's just about gone. We'll have purtnear two hours 'fore the full moon comes up to gather that herd of bred heifers," said Hayden Chaney, the gunslinger.

"Yeah, but the bossman wants 'em 'cross the river 'fore then," commented Wheeler.

The fourth member of their group, Posey Sitterly, trotted up and pulled rein. "Only two night guards ridin' herd."

"Sounds good…Chaney you take the one on the west, Hargrove, the east…Let's ride."

Wheeler spurred his claybank gelding down the hillside toward the herd. The others followed.

At the bottom of the hill, they split up. Chaney and Hargrove headed toward the guards. Wheeler and Sitterly circled around to the south side to be in position to drive the beeves north to the Red.

The night guard laid his Winchester across the front of his saddle and shook some tobacco from his bag of Bull Durham into a piece of rolling paper. He dropped his makings and twisted in his saddle when he heard the soft footfalls of a horse.

"Who the hell're you?" the Bar M rider said as he lifted his rifle and pointed it at the stranger barely visible in the last vestiges of twilight.

"Funny you should ask…I'm the man what's fixin' to blow yer ass outta that saddle," hissed Chaney

"What in hell?" The night guard levered a round into the chamber. "This Winchester's pointed at your gut, mister."

Chaney's grulla was angled directly at the man. The gunfighter eased his hand down to the butt of his Colt in the darkness. He rotated the bottomless swivel-holster horizontal, cocked and fired in one motion. The .45 caliber slug caught the cowboy in the middle of his chest with the unmistakable sound of a bullet striking flesh.

The Bar M rider flipped backward out of his saddle to the ground with a thud. His startled horse shied to the left and disappeared into the darkness.

The gunfighter looked down at the inert form, smiled and spat a stream of tobacco juice to the ground. "Pore bastards never see it comin'."

He pulled his pistol from its holster, ejected the spent shell, replaced it with a round from his belt and stuck it back home.

Gifford Hargrove was waiting in the shadows only twenty yards from the east side night guard with his Henry rifle centered on the man's back. He heard Chaney's shot almost a quarter-mile away and calmly squeezed the trigger.

The Bar M guard slumped forward in the saddle draping his arms on both sides of his mount's neck. The horse panicked at the sudden sound of the gunfire and his rider's movement, and then sprinted off back toward the ranch headquarters.

"Dammit," said Hargrove as he watched the animal disappear into the night.

BLUE WATER WOMAN

ROARING RIVER

Captain Bryan picked up the coffee pot with one of his deerskin gloves folded over for a hot pad. "Anybody need a refill?"

He glanced around at the others seated on rocks or logs near the fire.

Doctor Ashalatubbi held up his blue and white speckled graniteware cup. "Just barely run it over, Captain." He glanced to the east just above the tops of the trees at the edge of the full moon just making its appearance. "The strawberry moon is rising." He smiled. "It'll be almost bright enough to read by tonight and tomorrow night."

"What's the Indian story about the healing waters of the springs, *Anompoli Lawa*?" asked Fiona.

"Well I suppose it's as good a time as any to tell you since everyone is already sitting around the campfire with their coffee."

The cavalry officer sat the pot back on a flat rock close to the fire and took a seat next to Fiona to listen to the great Chickasaw Shaman.

Lawa took a sip from his cup. "You do make good coffee, Fiona."

"Thank you, kind sir."

"You see, the word *Shaman* simply means *storyteller*…or historian. Storytelling is the oldest form of communication, education and healing known to man. It actually dates back to

53

the dawn of mankind when stories were painted or drawn on the walls of caves or on animal skins in hieroglyphs or told around campfires...like this one. Later, when tools were developed, the images were carved in stone...petroglyphs, if you will."

"Like the carvings in ancient Egypt," said Bill.

"Even further back with Sumerian cuneiform...the earliest known system of using symbols. Its origins can be traced back to about 8,000 BC and maybe further."

"Really?" exclaimed Captain Bryan. "That's at least 4,000 years before the great pyramids."

"Exactly...But, before that, the oral tradition far predated the written word. In fact, the Twelve Tribes of Israel used the oral tradition for many centuries in passing down the parables of the creation and Noah's flood...It was not until King Solomon...the son of David and Bathsheba...decreed that these stories be written down, that we had any records from which much of the Old Testament was taken."

"And the aboriginal peoples of North America had the same traditions...Interesting," commented Fiona.

"That's true. Our story of the healing waters was when *Chi-hóo-wa*h, the Great Spirit, had completed his labors in creating the earth...he found a place to rest in the lush forest surrounded by flowers, songbirds and small animals..."

Fiona and the others leaned forward toward the elderly shaman, listening intently to his story.

"...Then a fierce, horned, fire-breathing dragon came out of the ground, disturbing the Great Spirit's slumber. The evil beast devastated the forest and brought disease and famine to *Chi-hóo-wah's* people. They pleaded with him to subdue the malevolent dragon and a great battle ensued..."

"What happened?" asked Bill.

Anompoli Lawa smiled. "I'm getting there, don't rush the story..." He took another sip of his coffee, and then continued, "The Great Spirit was victorious, and then he used all his powers to bury the savage beast deep in the earth...We can occasionally feel the ground tremble and shake with the dragon's rage at being trapped to this very day.

"Once *Chi-hóo-wah* had reclaimed his resting place and healed the land, he caused pure water to gush from the ground." Winchester waved his hand toward the river. "He decreed that this place and the purlieus would be forever sacred and that all could share in its healing waters."

"Purlieus?" asked Bill.

Doctor Ashalatubbi glanced over the top of his cup. "Surrounding area."

"Oh, got it."

A piercing roar reverberated through the surrounding dark forest. Everyone except *Anompoli Lawa* jumped, several spilling their coffee.

"What in the world?" exclaimed Fiona as she set her cup down and put her hand on the butt of one of her pistols.

"I would surmise it's *Lofa*...the great hairy man-beast of the forest...a disciple of the evil dragon."

The echoes had just died away when shrill cries cut the cool night air. The four looked up at the full orange moon and saw the silhouettes of two giant bald eagles pass over its face. They screamed again.

BAR M RANCH

Cookie Martindale, the ranch trail cook, cleaned the wound in Angel Gonzalez's upper back. "Lucked out, Angel. Bullet bounced off'n yer shoulder blade. Jest gonna take a few stitches."

"No, Señor Cookie...lucked out would be if Angel...didn't get heet at all," he managed to grunt out through gritted teeth between stitches.

"You think it was the Flying A bunch?" asked Arley Carter.

Angel turned his head slightly and glanced up at the ranch ramrod with a white bandage around his head. "Couldn't tell, *Jefe*. I see no one."

"They shot Slim from the front...Right in the heart. Looked to be close. His Winchester was on the ground next to the body...I'm thinkin' he had it in his hand when he was shot...They was a round in the chamber and the hammer was full cocked...The brass we found less than twenty feet away was a .45 Long Colt...Those two facts tell me it was a handgun," said Carter.

"Sounds like a shootist to me," said Flint Horton, one of the wranglers. "Better go git Sheriff Durbin."

"You go, Flint, you brung it up...I don't want no part of that lady law deputy of his." Arley gingerly touched the side of his head where his left ear used to be.

BLUE POOL

Winchester Ashalatubbi led the others into the large clearing next to the one hundred foot diameter clear blue spring. The ice cold water flowed away to the southwest as part of the headwaters of the White River.

"Wow!" exclaimed Captain Bryan. "What makes it so blue?"

"Because the pool has no known bottom is what gives the water its appearance. It's actually quite clear, as you will see," said Ashalatubbi.

He glanced over to the far side of the clearing at two elderly Indians dressed in beaded white ceremonial buckskins standing next to a twelve foot diameter dome-shaped wickiup covered with deerskins.

"*Sheeah!*" Winchester held up his right hand.

"*Sheeah, Anompoli Lawa,*" the two men answered with similar gestures.

Fiona and Jim traded curious glances as they dismounted following Doctor Ashalatubbi's lead.

Winchester and the other two Indians exchanged tribal handshakes of grasping each other's forearms with the right hand and the same side shoulders with the left.

He turned to Fiona, Bill and Captain Bryan. "Let me introduce my friends...*Kuukuh Ch'ayah,* Water Turtle, and *Hahtinu' U'ush,* Red Owl, of the Caddos. They're tribal spiritual leaders or Shamen, like me...Gentlemen, this is Deputy Fiona Miller...Deputy Marshal Brushy Bill Roberts and Captain Bryan of the United States Cavalry."

The same handshakes were exchanged.

"I'll picket the horses," the cavalry officer said.

"Fiona, you did bring a fresh camisole, didn't you?"

She frowned in confusion at Doctor Ashalatubbi. "I did, why?"

He pointed at the deerskin-covered lodge that resembled an upside down bowl. "This is what we call a sweatlodge...You'll recall I mentioned sending a telegram before we left Gainesville. It was to my counterparts here to set up the facilities and prepare for the ceremony."

"Ceremony?"

Ashalatubbi nodded. "Since you and I were the only ones to have visions when we touched the artifacts, I thought it best we go through our ceremony inside the sweatlodge...The experience should enhance that relationship and the visions.

58

Normally it's restricted to warriors, but, because of the circumstances, I think an exception is in order, plus, I think you qualify as a warrior...We will clean the skull and the necklace in the pure water first, and then take them inside with us."

The front of the structure had a loose hide flap over a small opening just big enough for a person to crawl through.

Six feet in front of the opening was a closely-packed ring of round, stream-tumbled granite rocks, each at least the size of a cantaloupe. The circle was half-again as large as a number two wash tub and had a roaring fire of hickory and pecan wood in the center. There were deerskins placed on either side of the ring.

"When the fire burns down to hot coals and stops smoking, we'll lift the lodge up and set it over the circle of stone. Red Owl and Water Turtle have already blessed the rocks which came from the White River."

Anompoli Lawa removed a Chickasaw breechclout of soft, tanned deerskin from his carpet bag. "Excuse me, I'll go into the bushes and put this on...Fiona, you should do the same with your camisole. I brought a specially blessed ointment to rub on our skin."

He handed the skull and necklace to Water Turtle. "*Kuukuh Ch'ayah*, would you please cleanse and sanctify these relicts in the pure water of the spring."

"It shall be done, *Anompoli Lawa*."

A few minutes later, Fiona and Winchester came back into the clearing. *Anompoli* was naked except for the breechclout and she was wearing only a white camisole which did little to hide her shapely figure.

Water Turtle took the ointment and applied it to Fiona's back after he had finished with Doctor Ashalatubbi.

"Smells like cinnamon and cloves with a touch of peppermint," she said.

"That's a start...It will help in the purification process...Turn around to the front so he can do it and your legs too," said Winchester.

At *Anompoli Lawa's* direction, Jim, Water Turtle and Red Owl picked up the lodge and set it over the circle of rocks and skins. The fire was down to red hot coals.

Red Owl crawled through the deerskin flap to purify the air inside the lodge and ward off evil spirits with a smoking sage wand.

Water Turtle handed him a wooden bucket of blessed water from the spring through the doorway to set inside—there was a porcelain dipper hung on the bail. He then passed a terra cotta bowl containing a thick brownish liquid to Red Owl. The Caddo Shaman set the bowl on one of the deerskins next to the stones and exited the lodge.

BLUE WATER WOMAN

Fiona and Doctor Ashalatubbi got down on their hands and knees and crawled through the small opening—the flap closed behind them. They sat cross-legged on the hides on opposite sides of the rocks. He placed the skull in front of his legs and the necklace in front of Fiona's.

Winchester handed her the bowl. "Drink half."

Fiona smelled of the liquid. "Oh, good God! What's in this?"

"You don't want to know…Drink it, quickly, and then we need to go into a meditative state."

Fiona drank some of the pungent liquid, gagged, but managed to keep it down. She handed the bowl back to *Anompoli Lawa*.

He drank the remaining potion, and then poured three dippers of the holy water on the hot rocks. They hissed and popped as steam boiled upwards and rapidly filled the small dome.

They could feel the heat emanating from the eons old granite rocks. An ethereal glow—different from the red hot coals—and without any apparent genesis, slowly brightened the thick cloud of steam.

Multicolored lights began to swirl about and pulsate to the same rhythm as their heartbeats. After a moment, he repeated the process as the rocks had heated back up. The moist heat was stifling. Then there was a bright light.

Fiona and *Anompoli Lawa* felt themselves rise out of their bodies and float in the white cloud—they could no longer feel the heat. There was no up or down. Their bodies were pure spirit.

There was a montage of images swirling about—Spanish conquistadors, a long line of laden burros, piles of blue and wine pearls, stacks of gold ingots and Indians with great white wolves, bald eagles and panthers.

An Indian maiden in a light blue beaded doeskin dress stood before a group of four kneeling Indians, two men and two women. As she poured a stream of water from a ceremonially decorated gourd, their eyes turned from dark brown to a bright antique gold.

They saw a figure materialize through the aromatic steam. It was a Catholic nun in a blue habit.

"Who are you?" Fiona asked.

"I was known as Sister Mary of Jesus of Ágreda. I was the Abbess of Ágreda...I visited the Atakapan Tejas of the Caddos many times long ago to convert them to Christianity through our Lord and Savior, Jesus Christ, using what you call bilocation. I came to the colonies in spirit form, transported by the aid of the angels."

"I can understand why *Anompoli Lawa* is seeing you...But why am I?"

"That crucifix you wear was my gift to my young niece in Italy over two hundred years ago…She was your great grandmother."

Fiona felt for the white gold and diamond antique cross hanging about her neck and looked down at it.

"You became my connection when you picked up the skull of my favorite acolyte *Bánushah Kuukuh Náttih*."

"The Blue Water Woman," said *Lawa*.

"Yes, she was very special to me and to her people. Her spirit is unsettled and now roams and is activating the protective spirits I taught her to use."

"Therianthropy…Shapeshifting," muttered the Shaman.

"Yes, *Anompoli Lawa*…when *Bánushah Kuukuh Náttih's* resting place was disturbed, her entity became viable again and recruited some descendants of the Caddo to metamorphose them into lycanthropes. Now they are expanding into other forms as she feels is necessary."

"Eagles," said Fiona.

"Yes…and there will be other creatures. These altered states can become permanent the longer the violation goes without being corrected."

"You mean the transformed giant wolves won't be able to return to human form?" she asked.

Another figure materialized out of the multicolored mists…It was the same beautiful Caddo maiden with long dark hair and antique gold eyes that had been pouring the water over the four other natives. She was wearing the cowrie shell, lapis lazuli necklace about her neck and a white underfeather from a bald eagle hanging from her tresses adjacent to her right ear.

"You must help us," the acolyte said in a voice that was like liquid silk. "Once the creatures become permanent, they will consider all mortal humans as enemies and desecrateors who have profaned our sacred land…I will not be able to stop them. My remains and all other items taken must be sanctified and returned."

The nun raised her hand. "There is an evil person behind this desecration you must…"

The images of Mary of Jesus of Ágreda and *Bánushah Kuukuh Náttih* began to fade as the mists and steam dissipated.

"Wait," Fiona shouted. "Please don't go. Who is this person? We…"

They were gone as the steam faded away. Fiona and *Anompoli Lawa* looked at each other for a long moment.

"We will receive no more." He nodded toward the doorway.

She rose to her hands and knees, crawled past the deerskin flap and stood erect in the bright sunlight when she was outside. Winchester followed right behind her.

Kuukuh Ch'ayah and *Hahtinu' U'ush* simultaneously dowsed both of them with buckets of ice cold water from the spring.

Fiona screamed and jumped up and down. "Oh, my God! That's freezing! Why did you do that?"

Anompoli Lawa wrapped his arms about his bony chest and shivered. "To cleanse our souls, my child, and bring us back to reality."

Water Turtle and Red Owl handed each of them blankets they instantly wrapped about their shivering bodies.

"What did ya'll see?" asked Captain Bryan. "We could hear you talking to someone inside there."

"I'm going to get dressed first, then I'll tell you what we saw...though you won't believe it...Not sure I do."

"The eye sees only what the mind is prepared to comprehend," said *Anompoli Lawa*.

Jim handed Fiona and Winchester cups of coffee as they walked into the clearing back in their clothes. They gave him their damp blankets.

She took a sip and rolled the hot cup between her palms. "Umm, that's good...I don't think I've ever felt anything quite so cold as that water."

"I can relate to that," said Bill. "I bathed in it to treat my leg while you and Doctor Ashalatubbi were inside the lodge."

"How did it work?" she asked.

He walked a small circle without his cane. "Almost no pain at all from *Kuruk*'s bullet wound or Doctor Williford's surgery now…and he said he had to dig around in there hunting for the ball like he was harvesting potatoes."

"See?" said Ashalatubbi.

Fiona stretched her left arm and rotated her shoulder. "Oh, my goodness. My shoulder is so much better, too…Must have been the dousing."

"It's not so much about what we get that makes life worth living…but what we give." *Anompoli* looked up to see the unusual sight of the sun in the eastern sky chasing after the full summer solstice strawberry moon in the western sky. "An appearance I will only see once in my lifetime…It is good."

Water Turtle and Red Owl had moved the sweatlodge from over the fire pit and wrapped the sanctified artifacts in a blessed white butter-soft doeskin, tied it with thongs and placed it in Winchester's carpet bag.

Everyone sat cross-legged around the rekindled fire pit to listen to Fiona and Winchester tell about their experience.

"Well?" Bill looked first at Doctor Ashalatubbi, and then at Fiona.

"It was amazing. I never knew…" said Fiona.

"The mystics call it an esoteric astral projection experience…The Navajo call it skinwalking…and the Muscogean tribes call it spirit-walking," said *Anompoli Lawa*. "It is the place between the physical body and that of therianthropy or shapeshifting."

66

"I felt like I was falling and floating at the same time looking down at my body still sitting next to the ring of rocks...We saw and talked to images of Mary of Jesus and the Blue Water Woman...They were as real as anyone sitting around this fire...It's something I'll never forget."

"It's entirely possible you may have to do it again at some point."

Fiona took a deep breath. "At least I'll have an idea of what it's all about...and prepare for the ice water soaking."

Winchester chuckled. "I've done the ceremony many times in my life and believe me, my child...you're never ready for the water cleansing after the heat of the lodge."

She nodded, and then stated, "I still don't understand why those two young people were desecrating the sacred site."

Ashalatubbi took a sip of his coffee. "It is for us to figure out. You'll recall the images we saw before Mary of Jesus of Ágreda and *Bánushah Kuukuh Náttih* appeared?"

"Yes, there were pack-laden burros, Spanish conquistadors, piles of blue and wine pearls and stacks of gold ingots..."

"I think there's our answer," said Winchester.

"But, you didn't find out where the treasure was," commented Bill.

"No...But, it doesn't really matter. It can't be touched. We must find out who is searching for it and stop them."

"What if they've already found it?" asked Captain Bryan.

Anompoli Lawa and Fiona exchanged glances.

"Then we may have a problem that is far beyond our comprehension and ability to solve," said the Shaman.

"You mean if the shapeshifters become permanent?" asked Bill.

"Not only that, but we don't know how many there are…or will be." *Lawa* looked at everyone sitting around the sacred ring of rocks.

They heard shrill screams and looked up as two great bald eagles lifted off from the top of a huge burr oak at the edge of the clearing and circled the pool.

"We may have some time, yet," commented *Anompoli Lawa* as he watched the creatures soar away.

§§§

CHAPTER FOUR

BAR M RANCH

Walt Durbin sat on a stool next to Angel Gonzalez's bunk with a tin cup of bunkhouse coffee in his hand. The Mexican cowhand was laying on his side to avoid putting pressure on his back wound.

Ramrod Arley Carter, wrangler Flint Horton and several other hands stood around or sat on nearby bunks.

"So, yer sayin' you didn't see nothin', that right, Angel?"

"No, Señor Sheriff, see nothing. Only hear shot from the other side of the herd an' then something heet me in the back...Is all Angel remembers till he wake up here in the bunkhouse."

"We heard Buster gallop into the headquarters and he was standing outside the corral gate when we come out of the bunkhouse," said Flint.

"He is good horse," grunted Angel.

"Either that er he was hungry," said Arley as he handed Walt the brass he had picked up. "Found this next to Slim's body...we tracked the herd to the river. No tellin' where they come out."

Walt looked at the shell casing, pitched it up in the air, caught it and slipped it in his vest pocket. "A shootist." He turned to the ramrod. "How many they get?"

"Seventy-nine, Sheriff...Our entire herd of replacement bred heifers. Add that to our mama cows they been gittin' over the last three months an' that means no calf crop next year."

"And that just about takes us outta the cow business."

They all turned to see the sixty-five year old, lanky owner of the Bar M, Russ Marker, standing in the doorway. He stuck his rosewood pipe in his mouth, took an easy draw, exhaled blue smoke and continued,

"Unless we get our stock back..." He looked around at the hands in the bunkhouse. "...gonna have to let everybody go and sell the ranch just to pay what I owe. The bank is leanin' on me real hard...I'm afraid it's one of the vicissitudes of life."

"How many acres do you have, Mister Marker?" asked Walt.

"Little over three thousand, straddlin' the Cooke and Montague County line all the way to the Red."

"Good size place," said the sheriff.

Marker nodded. "If we were runnin' a stocker operation, but we got a breedin' setup...Top of the line stock. Been crossin' the native Longhorn with Hereford an' Angus...Took fifteen years to git 'em to where I wanted 'em an'...now they're gone...Too damn old to start over."

"An' you think it might be the Flyin' A bunch?" Walt looked at Arley.

Carter looked at the floor embarrassed and shuffled his feet. "Naw...Jest had a bit too much to drink at the Silver Dollar an' was pissed on account they're not losin' any stock...Don't make no sense." He glanced at his boss.

"Their place is east and south of you, right?"

Marker nodded. "They're in the Cross Timbers and the blackland gumbo. Good for raisin' feed...sorghum, oats and such...They're into stockers."

"Who's wantin' yer place?"

The owner almost chuckled. "The bank mostly...But, had a couple of shyster lawyers been makin' runs at me over the last six months...Their offerin' price goes down every time they come out."

71

Walt rubbed the back of his neck, took a sip of his coffee and shook his head. "Uh, cold…Their offers didn't happen to be around the same time as you losin' stock?…Were they?"

"Son of a bitch, now that you mention it." Russ took a hard draw on his pipe, looked in the bowl, popped it in the palm of his calloused hand a couple of times and pitched the ashes out the door behind him.

"Don't suppose you know who they were representin'?" asked Walt.

Marker shook his head. "That's the way it is with those jake-legged bastards. They don't give a jot or a tittle 'bout right or wrong…just don't want to lose their cut."

Durbin got to his feet, stepped over to the potbellied stove in the center of the room and filled his cup from the blue merle graniteware pot on top. "Well, I'd say it's obvious that somebody wants yer place, Mister Marker, an' er tryin' to drive you to bankruptcy to git it on the cheap."

Russ stuck his empty pipe in his shirt pocket, paused, then nodded. "Hmm, think meby you're right, Sheriff."

RED RIVER BOTTOM

Hayden Mayweather and Rash Herron pushed through the brush to a game trail that paralleled the river.

"Dang, dadgum whoa vines eat a feller plumb up," said Hayden.

"Druther have whoa vines than dewberry vines any day, was me," added Rash as he pulled one of the tough, thorny vines loose from his faded Levis.

The two friends looked up and down the two-foot wide trail.

"Well, whichaway you wanna go?"

Rash studied the ground in both directions. "Damn-if-I-know...Don't see no wolf tracks atall."

"Well 'cordin' to my cousin at the undertaker's, it was 'posed to been some kinda monster wolves what kilt them two kids...You know how much a good wolf hide'll bring?"

"Hell, yeah...Least thirty er forty dollars, I 'spect."

"What do we do with these here marbles we found back yonder?" Hayden pulled nine blue pearls from his pants pocket and looked at them.

"Give 'em to yer boy. Don't he play marbles?"

"Yeah, could...Funny, wonder how they got in that pile of dirt with them bones, anyway?"

"Somebody musta buried 'em with whoever that was. Probably a kid what died an' they was his." Hayden looked off to their right as he pocketed them. "Let's head down toward the river. They's a lotta pecan trees down there."

"You think them wolves'll be there?"

"Hell, I don't know…It's jest lots easier to walk an' hunt there 'cause them bigassed trees shade the ground and don't let the briars grow."

Rash nodded. "Makes sense to me."

They moved off downslope toward the slow-moving Red and into the dense stand of large pecan and hickory trees.

"There should be bunches of squirrels in here an' they'd be good food fer wolves," said Hayden.

"Meby they done et 'em all an' that's why they jumped them kids…don'tcha see?"

"Rash, sometimes yer bread jest ain't real done, you know that?"

"What'er you talkin' 'bout?"

"Cousin Smead said they wasn't et, jest their throats tore out."

"Well, meby they was jest savin' 'em fer later…Ever thank 'bout that?"

Hayden spun around. "What was that?"

Rash looked all about the surrounding dark woods. "What?"

"Thought I seen somethin' over yonder." He pointed at a thick copse of willows down close to the river. "You loaded?"

"Well, yeah…Thank my mama raised a fool?"

Mayweather glanced over at his smaller friend as the man checked the chambers of his double-barreled twelve gauge, pulled two cartridges from his shirt pocket and quickly slipped them in.

"You really don't want me to answer that."

There was a flash of white on the other side of the clump of willows.

"There, I seen it again." Hayden fired his single-shot .410 at the shadowy brush.

Rash pulled both triggers of his old Greener in the same general direction. "You missed, peckerwood!"

"By the Lord Harry, did you see that thang?" Mayweather put another shell in his gun.

"Hell...was shootin' at it wadn't I?"

"Oh, God, look!" Hayden pointed at a set of golden eyes looking at them from the shadows.

"Shit! There's another over thataway." Rash saw another set coming through the trees to their left.

"An' there!" Mayweather fired his .410 shotgun back behind them.

The two men stood back-to-back with their heads either on a swivel or looking down at their empty firearms as the mysterious golden eyes closed in from all four sides...

GAINESVILLE DEPOT

The sun was just setting as Fiona, Bill, the Captain and Winchester waited back at the livestock car. They watched while the hostlers unloaded their mounts, under the direction of a portly yard manager with a stub of an unlit cigar in his mouth.

"Easy with that mule, boys. Deputy Miller is a bit partial to him...Plus if'n you jerk him about, he's libel to take a plug outta your shoulder for you. He don't tolerate no sass...an' she don't neither."

"Yep, talking about you again," said Bill.

"'Words, words, mere words, no matter from the heart'," said Fiona.

"Shakespeare."

She glanced at him. "Very good, Sir Bill."

"'Better a witty fool than a foolish wit'."

She cut her eyes at him. "Don't push it."

They turned as Sheriff Durbin walked up from the direction of the depot.

"Walt, didn't know you were going to meet us."

"Thought I might as well, Fiona."

"You look a bit stressed, something wrong?" asked Bill.

"Could say that..." He cleared his throat. "Had two more killin's up in the river bottom this mornin'."

"What?" exclaimed Captain Bryan.

"Same type?" asked Winchester.

Walt nodded. "Couple local hunters, Hayden Mayweather and Rash Herron...throats tore out. No other wounds. We done brought 'em in to the undertakers."

"How did you..."

Walt looked at Fiona. "Mayweather's wife come by the office, saying her husband an' Rash went huntin' fer wolves up in Frog Bottom an' swore on a stack of Bibles they would be back by noon...They wasn't. So me, Bodie and one of my new deputies went lookin' for 'em...Found 'em purty close to where ya'll found the kids." He reached in his coat pocket, pulled out an envelope and handed it to Fiona. "Found these in Mayweather's pocket."

She opened it and poured out nine blue pearls into her hand.

"Oh, Lord," said Doctor Ashalatubbi as he glanced over. "They must have found the mound."

"Or another one," said Fiona.

Winchester removed his black tall-crowned hat, wiped his brow with his handkerchief, and then put it back on. "There's no telling how many mounds there are in the area," he added.

"Glad we brought several canteens of water from the spring," commented Bill.

"We may need them all," said *Anompoli Lawa*.

"I assume ya'll accomplished your mission."

Fiona nodded. "Could say that, Walt, could say that. Fill you in when we get to Faye's...Anything else been going on while we were gone?"

"Oh, yeah."

SKEANS BOARDING HOUSE

"Well, Walt, that's pretty much the story...Just have to figure out who it was she was talking about," said Fiona.

"Lordy, lordy, lordy." He shook his head, got to his feet and paced around the parlor, and then sat back down. "That mighta scared me plumb to death...Heard some of the same kinda stuff from the Tawakonis down in central Texas...You know, sweatlodge visions, shapeshiftin' an' the like. Always figured it was just myths and campfire stories."

"Afraid not, Walt. It's something I'll remember for the rest of my life."

"All myths and legends have a basis in fact somewhere along the line," said Doctor Ashalatubbi.

"I have to go out to the Bar M tomorrow to scout around for clues on that rustlin' an' killin'...Ain't one thang it's another."

"Goes with the territory." Fiona stared at the cold ashes in the fireplace for a moment and spoke again, "Walt, you said the Bar M straddles the Cooke and Montague County line, right?"

He nodded. "Uh, huh."

She turned to Winchester. "How far west did the Atakapan Tejas and Caddo territory extend?"

"Just the other side of the Chisholm Trail in Montague County. Why?"

"Not sure. It's just my instincts are screaming that all this is tied together…somehow or someway. Think I'll go out with you tomorrow…If that's all right?"

"Shore. Use all the help I kin git. Yer still deputized anyhoo."

"Count me in," said Bill.

"I'll go, too," chimed in Bodie.

"And me," added Captain Bryan. "Glad it's not till tomorrow. Need to spend some time with Ruth Ann."

The little girl looked up from the floor where she was playing with the babies. "Did you say something to me, Daddy?"

He glanced at her and grinned. "No, baby, not really…Guess you're enjoyin' the twins?"

"Oh, yes…Cassie can almost say Ruthie." She giggled. "It comes out 'Ru-Re'."

Baby Cassie Ann was sitting up in front of Ruth Ann. She laughed and waved her arms up and down.

"Ru-Re...Ru-Re!" She reached one hand out for the older girl.

"That's so good, Cassie," Ruthie said, leaning over closer to the one-year old little girl.

Little Bass looked first at his sister, and then at Ruth Ann and got a half grin on his face.

"Looks like my son is goin' to be takin' after his namesake."

"How's that, Bodie?" asked Bryan.

"Ain't gonna talk till he's got somethin' to say."

Fiona laughed. "So true...And when he does, you better listen tight...because if he's truly like Bass Reeves, he won't be saying it twice."

"Sounds like he's a man I'd like to meet," said Jim.

"He is one of a kind," said Bodie.

"Say, not to change the subject, but when do you replace the sanctified remains and necklace?" asked Sheriff Durbin.

They all looked at the Chickasaw Shaman.

"Right. We never thought to ask," said Bill.

He cleared his throat. "Not until the next full moon...twenty-eight days from now."

"Oh, wonderful," mumbled Fiona.

"It's known as the Buck Moon."

"Buck Moon?" questioned the captain. "That's a new one on me. What's it mean, Doc?"

"The first full moon after the solstice is when deer begin to grow their new antlers…ergo the Buck Moon."

"Well, I'll be danged, learn somethin' ever day," said Walt.

"Confucius said, 'You cannot open a book without learning something'," said Fiona.

"Yes, but we don't have a book."

Fiona looked at the cavalry officer. "All life is a book…if we know how to read it."

Anompoli Lawa smiled and nodded. "Ah, so very true, my child."

BAR M RANCH

Walt led the small posse, consisting of one of his new deputies, R.J. Muller, along with Fiona, Marshal Roberts, Captain Bryan and Texas Ranger Bodie Hickman. They rode single file down the steep limestone escarpment into the Red River valley.

The ridge—once a reef in a shallow ancient sea that covered much of Texas and Oklahoma during the Paleozoic Era—paralleled the Red for almost sixty miles, well into Clay County to the west. The river's meandering journey to the east and eventual confluence with the mighty Mississippi, cut into the tertiary and alluvial deposits during the Pleistocene Epoch to form the wide fertile valley.

The Red ran north to south in this area after it passed Illinois Bend, where it curved back to the west toward Spanish Fort. The river bed cut back and forth across the four-mile wide valley, seemingly at a whim, creating gullies, arroyos, coolies, gulches and old horseshoe lakes.

The entire area during the great trail drive days was sometimes packed with up to sixty thousand head of longhorns waiting to cross at Red River Station, west of Illinois Bend—the main ford used on the Chisholm Trail.

"Where were those two Bar M cowhands shot?" asked Fiona.

Walt turned in his saddle and pointed off to the west. "Over yonder...See that swag between them two hog backs? Had the herd bedded down in the swale...Angel, the survivor ya'll met back at the headquarters, was on the east side over here and Slim Smith was on the west."

Durbin pulled rein once they got to the bottom and turned to face the others. "I mind it was fair easy to slip up on 'em...bein' below the ridges an' all."

Fiona raised up in her saddle and panned the entire valley. "You know, all these cliffs and rocks are limestone. Bet anything there are caves and caverns everywhere around here."

Walt glanced around also. "Could be. Not too familiar with this country, like I am around Austin and San Antonio. But, there's a lot of limestone down there too…They find caves all the time."

Walt pulled out a plug of Brown's Mule, bit off a chunk, and then continued, "I heard of one feller who was digging a new water well and broke through the top of a humongous cavern. Like to fell in…The original entrance got covered up somehow, so he had some neighbors lower him down with a rope." He spat a stream of tobacco juice off to his right. "Found all sorts of Injun artifacts as well as bones from some kinda big cats with real long teeth and them huge hairy elephants…"

"You mean smilodons or sabre-tooth cats and mastodons? They went extinct about ten thousand years ago…along with our friends the dire-wolves," said Fiona.

"You mean those giant wolf tracks we seen over in Frog Bottom?" asked Bodie.

"I do."

"If those monster wolves ain't extinct, then maybe them sabre-tooth cats ain't either."

"You may have a point, Bodie, except according to the Blue Water Woman, she's transforming some Caddo descendants into the creatures."

"You mean like magic?"

"No, Bodie, like Indian mysticism or spiritualism," said Bill.

"Ya'll are talkin' way over my head," commented Walt.

There was the sound of a bullet striking flesh, followed a little over a half second later by the boom of a rifle echoing through the valley. Deputy Muller, on the west side of the sheriff, cried out and tumbled from his saddle.

"Son of a bitch," exclaimed Walt. "Ride for that draw." He reined his blood-bay gelding, Pepper, to his right and spurred toward an arroyo that curled toward the river.

Fiona, Bill, Captain Bryan and Bodie quickly followed suit as more shots kicked up dust clouds from the ground around their mount's pounding hooves. The cavalry officer slumped over in his saddle.

They scrambled down to the bottom, some ten feet below the surrounding ground. Several bullets ricocheted from nearby boulders and whined off into the distance.

Fiona jumped off Spot. "Jim!" She ran toward his rented horse as it danced in fear from the sounds of the gunfire and grabbed its reins up close to the bridle.

The captain slowly slid from the saddle, landing on the ground at Fiona's feet.

Bill had dismounted and snubbed Tippy to a small bois d'arc tree eking out an existence at the edge of the draw. He ran over and took the reins of Bryan's horse from Fiona as she knelt down beside him.

"Jim…Jim?"

Gunfire continued to rain down on the gully from the ridge to the west…

SKEANS BOARDING HOUSE

Doctor Ashalatubbi placed the nine blue pearls on a clean piece of white cotton cloth that was next to a blue merle graniteware wash basin on the picnic table in the backyard. He picked up the pearls, one at a time, and gently placed them in the bottom of the pan.

He removed the cork from one of the canteens they had brought back from the Blue Pool in Arkansas and poured enough of the blessed water in the basin to cover the artifacts.

"Whatcha doin', Doctor Ashalatubbi?"

He turned at the sound of the voice to see little Ruth Ann Bryan standing beside him, staring at the pearls in the wash basin.

"Ruthie! Goodness, child, I didn't hear you walk up."

She giggled. "You were kinda busy and I didn't want to interrupt you."

"Well, you were certainly successful…As to what I'm doing. I'm sanctifying these ancient Indian artifacts."

She looked closer at the pearls. "What's sanc-ti-fying?" she asked very slowly, making sure she was properly saying the word.

"It means to purify and cleanse…to make holy or hallow. You see, these are special pearls that were dedicated by my people a very long time ago to our Great Spirit. We call him *Chí-hóo-wah*…In the Holy Bible, he is referred to as the Lord God, King of Kings, *Elohim, Yahweh, Adonai* and *Jehovah*."

"The last one you just said, *Jehovah*, sounds an awfully like what you said your people call him…*Chí-hóo-wa*h."

Anompoli Lawa smiled and nodded. "Yes it does…He is called by many names, but, there is only one god…the God of all."

He poured a little more water over the blue pearls and swirled them around in the bottom of the pan. "Some bad people have touched these and I have to make them sacred again before I can rededicate them to *Chí-hóo-wah*…and put them back in their resting place…Do you understand?"

She looked up at the gray-haired Indian Shaman. "I think so…They were a gift to God, somebody stole them and you have to clean them before you can give them back."

"Very good, Ruthie…That's very good."

"Can I help?"

Winchester thought for a moment, *Is there anything more pure than the innocence of a child?* "I think that's a marvelous idea, my dear...You take this clean cloth and I'll hand you the pearls one at a time...Dry them carefully and place each one in the middle of that piece of sacred white doeskin...all right?"

"Yes, sir...and thank you for letting me help."

He knelt down and hugged her. "No, child, It is I who thank you." He stood up, turned back to the basin, made the Indian hand signs for 'Friend' and 'Blessing' and reverently said, *"Chí-hóo-wah-bya-chi." Anompoli Lawa* handed Ruthie the first pearl.

A bald eagle voiced its piercing cry as it launched itself from the top of a one hundred foot loblolly pine that grew next to the carriage house.

Anompoli Lawa and Ruth Ann looked up as the huge raptor's wings lifted him toward the scattered clouds overhead.

"Well, I think we were being watched by one of *Chí-hóo-wah's* Guardians," said Winchester.

Ruthie's eyes followed the big bird as he caught a thermal and glided in a large circle over the boarding house. "Does he approve?"

She looked over at the Shaman as he watched the eagle, too.

"I would hope so, child. I would hope so." He picked up another pearl and handed it to her.

BAR M RANCH

Fiona stuffed her white handkerchief under Captain Bryan's shirt just above the top of his hip, below his ribs, and pressed it against the profusely bleeding wound.

His eyes fluttered and he groaned.

She instinctively ducked as a bullet cracked past her head and kicked up a cloud of sand behind her. "Jim, we've got to get to cover. Can you move?"

"Huh?"

"Can you move?"

"Uhhh…I can try."

He rolled over, moaned, and crawled on his hands and knees, with Fiona helping him, over to the bottom of the embankment of the gully on the west side.

"Now, stay there and don't move," she admonished.

"The thought never crossed my mind." He collapsed against the dirt wall with another moan.

Fiona got to her feet and sprinted down the arroyo to where Spot was tethered and jerked her .45-70 long-barreled Winchester from the boot. She crawled up the side of the gully to the base of a juniper growing just at the edge. Levering a round into the chamber, she jerked her hat from her head and peeked over the edge.

Bill, Bodie and Walt were spread along the top of the arroyo in various places of concealment south of her position and were returning fire with their rifles. She could see they were shooting at six separate clouds of gunsmoke on the boulder-strewn limestone ridge a little over three hundred yards to the west. It was apparent the drygulchers weren't changing positions—as they should have.

Fiona snapped a shot at the center of the northernmost cloud, and then rapidly working the lever, fired another one foot to the right and then one to the left. It almost sounded as if she only fired one bullet—like rolling thunder.

Bodie, the nearest to her, glanced over. "Jesus-all-mighty." He turned back and duplicated her maneuver, although not as fast.

She could hear Bill laugh through Bodie and Walt's gunfire.

"Told you."

After a couple of moments of the fusillade, the shots from the ambushers stopped.

"Well, either they're all shot to doll rags or they've lit a shuck," said Walt as he reloaded his Winchester with .44-40 rounds from his belt.

"Maybe both," commented Fiona as she got to her feet and made her way back down to Jim.

She knelt down. "How're you feeling, big guy?"

He moaned, and then grunted as he sat up. "Like I been shot."

"It's going to get worse."

He looked at the concern on her face. "How's that?"

"Bullet didn't go through. Doc Wellman's going to have to dig it out."

"Wonderful." He groaned again and laid back down.

"Bill and I are goin' to ride up there and see if there's a body count, after we check on Deputy Muller," said Walt.

Thirty minutes later, Walt and Bill rode back down into the gully and dismounted.

"Muller?" asked Fiona.

Bill shook his head. "Right through the heart…Dead when he hit the ground."

"Would'ov been me if'n he hadn't a been where he was…Looked like there were six bad guys shootin' at us from that ridge. Four of 'em got away…Had their horses picketed in a draw behind the ridge," said Walt.

"Recognize the two we hit?" asked Fiona.

Walt pulled his canteen from his saddle, brought it over and handed it to Captain Bryan. "Nope…Never seen 'em 'fore…Prob'bly from the Nations."

"Better build a travois for the captain," said Bill as he walked toward a clump of willows.

"No need," said Jim through clenched teeth. "Just help me on my horse…Believe I can make it to the ranch headquarters. 'Spect they got a buckboard there."

"Hardhead," muttered Fiona.

"I think it's obvious that somebody don't want us snoopin' 'round here," said Walt.

Fiona glanced at him. "There is nothing more deceptive than an obvious fact."

Bill grinned and nodded. "Arthur Conan Doyle."

§§§

CHAPTER FIVE

WELLMAN'S CLINIC
GAINESVILLE, TEXAS

Bodie and Walt sat nervously in the waiting room while Doctor Lucius Wellman performed surgery on Captain Bryan in another part of the clinic. Bill had gone over to the boarding house to inform everyone there, especially Ruth Ann, about her father.

Fiona came through the door to the kitchen carrying a tray with three mugs of steaming coffee. The men got to their feet.

"Thank you," said Walt and Bodie at the same time.

She sat the tray on a corner table after the two men grabbed their cups and sat back down. Fiona took hers and took a seat in a straight-backed chair next to the table.

BLUE WATER WOMAN

The front door opened and Ruth Ann rushed in, followed by Faye and Bill.

"My daddy! My daddy...Where's my daddy," she said through her tears.

Fiona quickly set her cup down, got to her feet, knelt down and hugged the little girl.

"Ruthie, he's with the doctor right now. Why don't you come over here and sit down?"

She pushed away from Fiona. "No! Get away from me...This is all your fault. He wouldn't have gotten shot if it weren't for you."

Ruth Ann spun around, crossed her arms, stared at the door that led to the surgery room and silently cried. Fiona and Faye exchanged glances.

The older woman bent over and held the child's shoulders in her hands and looked in her tear-streaked face. "Honey, it's not anybody's fault. Things like this..."

"Leave me alone!" She twisted away from Faye's hands as Doctor Wellman entered the waiting room and pulled his surgical mask down from his face.

Everyone shot to their feet...

NORTH COOKE COUNTY

Monte Wheeler drew rein in front of a black phaeton style Stanhope Sedan buggy with a closed back. The man in the shadows inside held the reins to a four stocking copper sorrel Standardbred mare.

He was wearing a three-piece suit with a dark gray pure beaver hat characterized by a single dent, called a gutter, running down the center of the crown with a pencil-roll two-inch brim—known as a Homburg. The silver-haired man was backlit by an isinglass window behind his head—a cloud of blue cigar smoke rolled out of the interior as he took a puff, exhaled and said, "Well?"

Wheeler cleared his throat. "Uh...well, you see, Boss, a bunch of fellers rode down the ridge whilst me an' the boys was a scoutin' fer caves...An' I see'd the sun glint off'n a couple badges an' figured it was the county sheriff an' a posse come to check on where them two Bar M hands got themselves kilt, when we taken that last herd..." He cleared his throat again.

"Get on with it man."

"Well, Chaney, he pulled out his Winchester and shot one of 'em out of the saddle. The others hightailed it down into a draw."

The man in the carriage threw his expensive Cuban cigar out into the middle of the road. "Jesus Christ...I'm surrounded by imbeciles."

"An' see, then they started shootin' back...Kilt Hargrove and Massey, so we figured it was time to quit swappin' spit, an' we cut out fer the Nations."

"Dumb bastards should have stayed there and killed them all," the man mumbled. "All right, you bunch of Newtons stay the hell away from the Bar M...for now."

Wheeler spat a stream of tobacco juice into the road. "What's a Newton?"

"Isaac...oh, hell, forget it. Get the rest of the boys and just stay on the north side of the river or better yet, work up toward the Arbuckles...There has to be more than what you've found so far."

"You got it, Boss." Wheeler spun his mount and kicked him into a lope in the direction of the Red.

The man turned the buggy around in the road and headed back to Gainesville.

WELLMAN'S CLINIC
GAINESVILLE, TEXAS

"How is he?" asked Fiona.

95

Wellman had a half-grin on his face. "Sore, but, not near as bad off as he could be."

"What do you mean, Doc?" inquired Walt.

"Well, that rifle ball ricocheted off the top of his hip bone and traveled up and around to his back. I found it just under the skin about two inches from his spine." He held up the misshapened piece of lead. "I just had to make a small incision in his back…and it popped right out." He grinned and shook his head.

"Sounds like he drew a pat hand from a stacked deck."

"That's pretty close, Bodie."

"Can I go see my daddy now?"

"I expect so, child…I gave him ether, he's awake, but, still a little groggy, I would say…."

Faye took Ruth Ann's hand and they headed to her father's room.

Faye pushed the door open and peeked in. Jim rolled his head to the side, blinked a couple of times and gave her a soft smile. She eased the door the rest of the way, Ruth Ann darted in and ran over to his bed.

"Daddy! Daddy!" She threw her arms around his neck and hugged him tight.

"Whoa, whoa…easy girl. Daddy's not quite up to snuff," he managed to slur out.

She released her hug and stepped back. "Oh, I'm sorry, Daddy. I was so worried...Did I hurt you?"

He reached his hand out to her, she grabbed it and held it with both hands.

"Not really, honey. It just kinda tweaked the stitches in my side a little."

Walt, Bill and Fiona stood just inside the doorway beside Faye and Doctor Wellman.

The captain looked up. "Hey, don't I at least get a peck on the cheek?"

Fiona smiled, stepped over to the bed and kissed his forehead.

Jim frowned and looked deeply into her steel-gray eyes. "What is it?"

She glanced away. "Nothing. I just didn't want to interrupt anything."

"Nonsense. You know..."

"Daddy, it's my fault."

He looked over at his daughter. "Your fault for what?"

Ruth Ann turned her head toward Fiona, and then looked at the floor. "I..." She continued to stare at the floor as her eyes filled and tears began to roll down her cheeks. "I was..."

"I don't understand, honey. What are you trying to say?"

The little girl spun on her heels, ran to Fiona and threw her arms around her waist. "I'm so sorry. I didn't mean those awful things I said...Please forgive me?" She looked up at the older woman's face.

The tears flowed from Fiona's eyes, too, as she knelt down and held Ruth Ann close. "It's all right, Ruthie...I know you didn't...I love you."

"I love you, too," she said as her little body shook with sobs.

"Will somebody please tell me what's goin' on?" asked Jim.

His daughter turned back to her father, bit her lower lip and finally said, "Daddy...I wasn't a very..." She looked back up to Fiona. "...a very nice person." Ruth Ann ducked her head.

"What?" Her dad wrinkled his forehead.'

She looked at her father again, took a breath and continued, "I...I blamed Fiona for you getting shot...I said...said it was all her fault."

"Oh, honey."

Ruth Ann looked up at Fiona again. "Will you please accept my apology?" The tears flowed down her face again.

Fiona knelt down and embraced the little girl. "Of course I will, darling...of course I will...We'll pretend it never happened...All right?" She took a small linen handkerchief from her sleeve, dried Ruthie's eyes and kissed each closed eyelid.

Fiona looked over the child's head at her father and subtly shook her head for him not to say anything. He nodded in return.

"You know, I bet your dad would like some of Martha's bone broth...He needs the nourishment."

Ruth Ann stepped back. "I'll get it." She turned, headed out the door and down to the kitchen.

Jim looked at Fiona a moment, and then smiled. "That was a wonderful thing you did." His eyes started to fill. "To have never had children yourself..."

"I had five younger brothers and sisters. My parents were wonderful teachers...They taught me that it was much easier to build a strong child than to fix a broken adult."

ARBUCKLE MOUNTAINS
CHICKASAW NATION

Deputy US Marshal Jack McGann nudged his red and white Overo paint gelding, Chief, up the game trail that ran alongside Honey Creek. He was accompanied by his big white wolf-dog, Son.

The creek flowed over Turner Falls just south of the large log house where he and his wife, Angie, lived. It would join with the Washita River, which would eventually flow into the Red.

Honey Creek bubbled out of a cave in the mountain to the west-southwest of the falls from a deep aquifer—the entire area was honeycombed with caves throughout the limestone formations.

"Well, Son, looks like we're strikin' out on bringin' some venison home fer supper." He glanced down at the rabbit he had hanging from the saddle horn. "Reckon this half-growed rabbit ain't gonna be enough fer a stew." He raised up in the stirrups and looked all around for any other game.

The big wolf-dog spun around twice, barked, and sat down beside the trail.

"Mind I shoulda brought my fishin' pole. Leastwise they's always fish in the creek…Angie's gonna have to cook up some ham from the smokehouse, er some of that elk sausage we made last winter…actually that don't sound too bad, does it?"

Son barked again, and then whipped his head around back to the north and growled.

The stocky, mustachioed lawman followed his dog's gaze. He could see three men with four horses a little over two hundred yards away. They were bunched behind a copse of dogwood trees.

Then he heard a screech that sounded like all three witches from Macbeth combined into one.

"Uh, oh, them boys have done crapped and fell back in it…Come on, Son."

He reined Chief in the direction of the cacophony of wails—and the men.

As he got closer, he could see the strangers trying to hide behind the trees and a couple of large boulders, dodging the fist-sized rocks being hurled their way simultaneously with the piercing shrieks.

He dismounted, ground tied his paint and slipped up behind a large dolomite boulder. "Mary! Mary, it's Marshal McGann. Stop chunkin' them rocks. Everthang's awright…Hear?"

"Go away," she screeched back. "Leave me be…Git them highbinders away from here." She bounced a rock off the trunk of a tree that ricocheted into one of the men.

"Ow!…Tell her to quit," he cried out.

"Jest stop chunkin', Mary. I'll see they don't bother you none."

An elderly, skin and bones woman with dirty long scraggly gray hair down to her nonexistent waist stepped out of a small entrance to a cave. She wore a mixture of animal skins and old flour sacks for clothing and held a rock in each gnarly hand. Her pale skin was difficult to discern because of the grime and filth.

Ken Farmer

"Git 'em outta here, Marshal. Ol' Mary don't want 'em around…it's a spell she'll cast on 'em, she will," she cackled, showing all three teeth left in her mouth. Her speaking volume was not any softer than her shrieks.

Jack eased away from the boulder, not taking his eyes from the crazy woman, until he got to where the three men were. "You fellers best git on outta here. Crazy Mary kin hit a dove on the wing with them rocks…an' she'll charge hell with a cup of ice water."

"Damnation, I wuz fixin' to plug the old sow," said Hayden Chaney.

Jack pierced him with eyes that were the same shade of brown as his medium-short hair. "You'll do no such a damn thang, pilgrim. That there cave is her home…Folks 'round here call it Wild Woman Cave."

"I kin believe that," mumbled Posey Sitterly, the smallest of the three.

The gunfighter's hand eased in the direction of his swivel holster. Chaney froze when he looked over at the golden eyes of Son staring at him not two feet away and heard the deep rumble coming from his throat.

"You touch that gun, mister and he'll take yer hand off up to the elbow…an' if that ain't a fact, God's a possum," Jack said softly.

Beads of sweat broke out on Chaney's forehead. "You keep that animal away from me...I don't like dogs."

McGann chuckled. "He knows...He don't like you much neither...Now you boys git the hell on outta here. This is private property...Mine."

"Uh...We cain't," said Wheeler.

"What do you mean, 'You cain't'?"

"One of our, friends, uh, Anson Parsons...uh, fell in a hole over yonder." He pointed back behind them.

"How the Billy Bob hell did he do that?"

Wheeler pulled his hat off and wiped his brow with his bandana. "He...uh, stepped off'n his horse to water a bush. We heard a holler an' he disappeared."

Jack walked over to a small sinkhole and peered down inside. Darkness swallowed up the rent in the limestone after about ten feet. "Hey, feller...you awright?"

"Naw, I ain't...Leg an' a arm's broke," came a voice from the blackness down below.

"Aw, damn," Jack raised back up and walked over to his horse. He shouted at the old woman. "Mary, got a feller hurt down a hole. We'll be gone soon's we pull him out."

Her answering screech sounded like two cats making love.

Jack led Chief over to the hole, untied his thirty-five foot braided rawhide reata and shook out the loop. He glanced over at the three men and pointed at Posey. "You git to go down an' tie this here lariat to yer friend."

"Why me?"

"On account of if'n you wuz any smaller, you'd have to stand twice to make a shadow...Now here." He flipped the loop at the man. "Slip this under yer arms an' my horse'll lower you down...Take the rope off an' put it under that feller's arms like you had it an' Chief'll pull him out." He dallied the free end around his saddle horn.

"What about me?"

"If you don't stop snappin' my garters, I'll leave you down there...Now scat." Jack pointed at the hole.

Posey grumbled and stepped over to the hole as Chief backed away, taking up the slack.

"Ease yer legs over the edge and we'll let you down."

"Go slow now...Awright?"

"Plan on it...Holler when you touch bottom."

Jack led the paint forward one step at a time until Posey shouted out,

"I'm down...I'm down."

"Heard you the first time," Jack yelled back. "Put the lariat on yer runnin' buddy."

"Awright...Done."

He turned to Chief. "Back up, boy, back up."

The paint tucked his nose to his chest and backed in a straight line until the top of the man's head showed at the edge.

"Easy, son, just a couple more steps." He clucked at him and the horse complied.

Wheeler and Chaney grabbed Parsons under the arms and lifted him out.

"Ow, ow…Easy on the arm, Chaney."

"Yeah, right," the squint-eyed gunslinger said.

"What'd he call you?" asked Jack.

"Uh, Chaney. Why?"

"Wouldn't happen to be Haden Chaney, would it?"

"What if it is?"

"Well, jest heard the name is all." Jack's eyes narrowed.

"Hey!" came a shout from the hole. "Ya'll gonna pull me outta here?"

"Sooner than later," said Jack, as he pitched the lariat back down the hole, waited a moment for Posey to slip it over his shoulders, and then clucked again at Chief to back up.

In a few seconds the man grabbed at the edge of the hole to pull himself out onto the bare rocky surface. He rolled over on his back and undid the reata, throwing the loop over his head.

"Damn, I hate dark places…Black as a banker's heart down there, but I could hear water a roarin'. I don't mean a little bitty trickle, I mean somethin' purtnear big as the falls...an' then when I yelled, they was echoes."

"Maybe it was ghosts, Posey," said Monte and he laughed.

"Tain't funny, Wheeler."

"What're you fellers doin' up here anyways?" inquired Jack.

Wheeler looked at the others, and then at McGann. "Uh, we was headin't to, uh, Ardmore, Marshal. Been a visitin' some kinfolk over to Hennipen an' wuz just a cuttin' through."

"Uh, huh...Well, you best git Parsons here to a doctor. They's a couple in Ardmore. Probably take the rest of the day to git there...Doctor Ashalatubbi over on Carter Street is a goodun, if'n he's back in town from a trip down to Gainesville."

Jack watched as they helped Parsons in the saddle, and then the four of them headed slowly down the mountain. He reined Chief over to Wild Woman Cave. The affected woman came out screeching at him.

"Whoa, Mary, dang it. They're gone." He held out the cotton tail. "Here's somethin' fer yer pot."

She cackled as she snatched it from his proffered hand. "Rabbit fer Mary, it is...He-he-he-he."

Son sat down next to Jack's paint and cocked his head at the wild looking woman.

"Sorry, them fellers bothered you."

"Bothered Mary did not...A spell it was Mary put...Evil men they are." The old woman waved her free hand around and spat a watery stream of noxious light brown fluid from her lip full of snuff. It hit a horned toad sitting on a pumpkin-sized rock nearby, covering most of its stubby little tail and one back leg.

"Find yeller metal...neither...He-he-he-he...Ol' Mary knows." She spun around and shuffled back into the interior swinging the rabbit at her side by its ears.

Jack frowned as her cackling faded into the darkness. "Yeller metal?"

SKEANS BOARDING HOUSE
GAINESVILLE, TEXAS

Winchester loaded his bags in the back of the buckboard parked out front of the house. Bill sat in the seat holding the reins to a bay mare with a single star in the middle of her forehead.

"Thanks for the loan of the carpet bag for the artifacts, Bill. Needed something to protect the doeskin until I bring everything back down at the next full moon."

"No problem, Doc. Not planning on going anywhere till we get this all wrapped up. Just hope we can keep folks out of the river bottom."

"Well, the creatures aren't really held to that immediate area, you know."

"Yeah, wonder how far they might go out from the river?"

"I would suspect there's no conceivable restriction. You recall the eagles that followed us up to Arkansas?"

Doctor Ashalatubbi stepped on the hub of the front wheel and clambered into the seat next to Marshal Roberts. He looked back over his shoulder at the house. Perched on the rooster weather vane atop the tallest roof ridge was a bald eagle.

"Speaking of which, look up on Faye's roof."

Bill glanced up at the magnificent creature who appeared to be looking back at him. "Right. See what you mean…Too bad you can't stay a little longer."

"Got to get back to Ardmore. I'm sure my waiting room is full to the brim. Plus, need to go out and check on my grand niece, Baby Sarah. Angie said she's been frettin' of late. May have to switch her to goat's milk."

Bill clucked at the mare and flicked the ribbons over her rump. "Come up there, Annie…How's Jack's leg?" he asked as they headed in the direction of the train depot, six blocks away.

"Pretty well healed. He has some muscle weakness from being in the cast so long…Glad it was his femur and not his knee that broke when Chief fell on him…Jack's picking me up at the station in Ardmore."

The big raptor lifted from the roof and with several beats of its powerful wings, soared off to the north.

MCGANN HOME
ARBUCKLE MOUNTAINS

Jack pulled rein at the pole coral next to the big red barn.

Son spun and looked up to the west at the steep hillside behind the log house.

"Whatcha lookin' at, Son?" Jack asked as he dismounted and started unwrapping the front latigo from the O-ring on the girth.

His eyes tracked where Son was staring and his jaw fell. "Well, I'll be damned an' double rectified."

He watched as another big white wolf/dog turned, jumped from the top of the boulder he was on and vanish into the brush. Jack finished unsaddling Chief and turned him into the corral with a couple of blocks of hay.

He looked back up the hill once more and headed toward the front porch of his house. "Come on, Son...Wonder what yer daddy's doin' back here?" Jack muttered.

The big animal didn't wait for Jack to open the gate in the white picket fence that surrounded the front yard, but cleared it with a bound, ran up on the porch, sat down and barked once.

The dark-green gingerbread screendoor swung open to allow Jack's wife Angie to step out—and slammed shut behind her. A two-year old little girl with cotton curls was holding on to her mother's dress with one hand and a chicken leg bone in the other she had been chewing on to ease her teething pain.

The attractive Irish woman with her long wavy flaming red hair tied in a low pony tail at the back of her neck slapped her thigh with a dish towel. "Well, it's back ye are, husband of mine an' I'm not seein' any game for supper."

"You're not goin' to believe what happened, woman of the house...I just saw Boy."

"Boy! Faith and is it daft ye are? He hasn't been around since he brought Son to ye two years ago, just before we adopted our sweet Baby Sarah...It was him, are ye sure?"

"No question 'bout it," Jack said as he climbed the steps to the porch, picked up their daughter, Baby Sarah, gave her a kiss on the forehead and set her back down.

He leaned over to give Angie a peck and she turned her cheek to him.

"That doesn't explain the game ye're not carrying, husband."

"I know, but there were some fellers up by Crazy Mary's cave I had to deal with before they tangled with her. One of 'em had fallen in a sinkhole so me an' Chief had to pull him out...he was busted up some. Recognized one of 'em as a gunhawk, but hadn't see'd no paper on 'im."

A look of concern came over Angie's face. "Do ye think it had somethin' to do with seein' Boy?"

He chewed on the bottom of his mustache for a couple of seconds. "Last time we see'd him was when we had that set to with those miscreants of Baldwin's, the Sartain twins, before we got married...It's like he only comes around when they's malefactors in the area...Crazy Mary said the men up by her cave wuz evil..." He chuckled. "Said she put a spell on 'em."

Angie stepped forward and gave Jack a hug. "It's sorry I am, husband, for chastising ye about the game...It's a fine man ye are." She leaned back and gave him a soft kiss on the lips. "I'll cut some elk sausage down an' bake some sweet potatoes for our supper."

"That sounds great, hon. I'm gonna grab a couple of cold biscuits and hook up the mules to the wagon..."

"Aye, it's havin' to pick up Uncle Winchester at the station...I had forgotten. I'll fix enough for him too."

TRAIN STATION
ARDMORE, CHICKASAW NATION

"Uncle Winchester, this way," shouted Jack at the elder Chickasaw practitioner as he stepped down from the train.

"Here, let me take those." Jack indicated the carpet bags Doctor Ashalatubbi had in each hand with his physician's black leather valise under his arm.

The Indian Shaman kept the carpet bag he had in his right hand, but let Jack take the other two.

"I'll carry this one...It's kind of special."

"You're the boss. Wagon's over here."

"I need to go by the office first."

"Thought as much," said Jack as he put the two bags in the bed of the wagon.

Anompoli Lawa held the other carpet bag on his lap after he had climbed aboard.

Jack looked over at the elderly Chickasaw. "Special, huh?"

"You could say that."

"Uh, huh...Just did..." He clucked twice at the matched pair of black-nosed Tennessee mules. "You know, I see'd Boy earlier today...just behind the house up on the side of the mountain.

Anompoli Lawa glanced over at Jack. "It's a sign the spirits are watching. I'll fill you in about what went on down north of Gainesville and what this bag is about when we get out to your house...I think you'll find it interesting." He patted the carpet bag on his lap.

Winchester opened the door to his clinic on Carter Street—there were only four men in the waiting room. His early thirties nurse, Abigail Martin, met him at the door. She was wearing a typical starched white nurse's uniform.

"Doctor Ashalatubbi...Oh, good. I wasn't sure you were coming by when you got in. I sent the others home...Told them to come back tomorrow. There was nothing serious...except that gentleman over there. He has a broken arm and leg...They need setting."

Anson Parsons, in one of the straight-back waiting room chairs, leaned his head against the wall in obvious pain.

"That's the feller I told you about on the way over here what fell down a sinkhole, Uncle Winchester," said Jack. "Name's Parsons as I recall."

"Kin you fix him up, Doc?" asked Wheeler.

"An' git a hurry on, too, old man," said Chaney.

Ken Farmer

Jack looked at each of the three men that were standing in the middle of the room, and then centered on the gunslinger. "Slick, I suggest you keep yer mouth shut. Doctor Ashalatubbi don't cotton to pushin'…an' neither do I."

Chaney's hand habitually worked toward his swivel holster until Wheeler touched his arm and shook his head.

"I'd pay attention to Wheeler, there sunshine." Jack's hand was casually resting on the butt of his Smith and Wesson .44 caliber Russian revolver on his right hip.

"Another time, lawman, another time," Chaney hissed.

"Suit yerself…I've been up the hill and over the mountain a time er two," answered Jack.

Doctor Ashalatubbi nodded at the injured man and walked toward a door being held open by his nurse. He handed her the carpet bag. "Yellow Bird, put this in my office. Be particular with it now…It has special tribal artifacts in it."

Wheeler and the others exchanged glances.

"Thought her name was Abigail," said Jack.

"That's her Christian name, her tribal name is *Foshi Lakna*…Yellow Bird."

"Ah…gonna have to start takin' notes on all ya'll names."

"Wait till you meet Alex Sixkiller, Ben's brother. He's just been sworn in as a new Lighthorse. He's got a tribal name long as your arm…*Yahash Losa Ombi Pisali*."

"What does that mean?"

"Black Buffalo Sees Rain."

"Think I'll jest call him Alex."

Winchester chuckled. "Bring him in here...Jack, I'll need you and one of these other gentlemen to help hold him...You know what I have to do."

"Oh, I do indeed, Uncle." He looked at Chaney and gave him a wry smile. "Come on, peacock, you look like you can strut sittin' down."

"Give 'em a hand, Hayden," said Wheeler.

The gunhawk glared at Jack and clenched his jaw.

The room was pierced by the shrill hunting cry of an eagle from outside overhead as they assisted the injured man into the doctor's treatment room. Jack had a puzzled look on his face as he glanced up, in contrast to *Anompoli Lawa's* wry grin.

§§§

CHAPTER SIX

MCGANN HOME
ARBUCKLE MOUNTAINS

Angie filled Jack and her uncle Winchester's coffee mugs and set the pot on a stone plate. They relaxed in slat-back rockers on the newly screened-in back porch, enjoying the cool of the gloaming and their coffee.

"Now, Uncle, what is it about those Indian artifacts ye were goin' to tell us," she said as she sat down in her rocker across from the two men. Baby Sara was asleep in her crib taking her after-dinner nap. Her bedroom was in the new south side addition to the house.

Thirty minutes later, the Chickasaw Shaman finished telling Angie and Jack about the lycanthropy killings across the Red and the metamorphosed eagles that had been following him—even up to the Blue Pool in Arkansas and back.

"Is shapeshifting just the belief of the Indians here in North America, Uncle?"

"Goodness no, Angie, child…It's even mentioned in the world's oldest extant literature, such as the *Iliad* and the *Epic of Gilgamesh* where deities induced the metamorph process or shapeshifting to certain mortals."

Jack scratched his chin, and then the back of his neck.

"What is it, husband?"

"Oh, just thinkin'."

"Thought is sometimes how we rehearse behavior…or should," said Winchester.

Jack nodded and glanced at the venerable physician. "Yep, I was jest thinkin' 'bout the behavior of those nabobs in yer office this afternoon."

"You mean other than Parsons screaming like a stepped on cat when I set his leg?"

"Yeah…Somethin' I didn't mention when I pulled his worthless ass outta that hole an' his runnin' mates took him down the mountain."

"What was that?" asked Angie.

Jack rubbed the back of his neck again. "Ol' Crazy Mary said somethin' 'bout they didn't find the yeller metal."

Anompoli Lawa sat up erect and almost spilled his coffee. "What?"

"I thought the same thing when she said it…What yeller metal?"

Winchester got up, paced in a tight circle twice and turned to face Jack. "When Fiona and I were in the sweatlodge, before we talked to Sister Mary and the Blue Water Woman, we saw myriad visions of Spanish conquistadors, a long line of laden burros, piles of blue and wine pearls, Indians with great white wolves, eagles and panthers…and stacks of gold ingots."

"Kiss a fat baby. I can relate to that from when you put me through that sweatlodge ceremony…"

"When ye were tryin' to get your mind back," Angie interrupted.

"Memory, Angiedarlin', memory…git it right."

She covered her mouth as she giggled.

He continued, "The visions of my father and brother were almost real enough to touch…and true. Meby it all has somethin' to do with me seein' Boy."

Angie crossed herself. "Saints preserve us."

Winchester paced again and took a sip of his coffee. "You know, the Atakapan Tejas and Caddo lands extended up through the Oklahoma territory to the Missouri River…and actually most all of the Mississippi basin."

"The mound builders ye mean?" said Angie.

The Chickasaw Shaman nodded. "They were part of the Mississippian culture."

He pointed toward the carpetbag near his feet containing the re-sanctified artifacts. "Except, since they didn't really consider the yellow metal or gold as functional or even valuable to their society, they wouldn't have placed it in their burial mounds like the pearls and other artifacts."

"So you think…"

Winchester interrupted Jack. "I think they stole the gold to punish the invaders, because the Spaniards seemed to worship it."

"…and they must have hid it…jest to spite 'em fer makin' their people slaves an' minin' fer 'em."

Son snapped his head up from between his paws and looked south through the screened wall toward the falls. A few seconds later the long mournful howl of a wolf echoed through the canyon outside the house.

"Sounds like Boy is singin' his song…Hadn't heard that in a while." Jack looked at Winchester. "Reckon he's actually one of them lycan…whatcha call 'ems?"

"Lycanthropes…and no. I think Boy is a spirit wolf…a messenger…and always has been…But, he is part of the therianthrope spirit world and has never been human…Of course, I could always be wrong."

"You reckon them four miscreants wuz involved with the goin's on down in Texas when Fiona an' them got shot at?"

Anompoli Lawa looked at Jack for a long moment. "What was it you said Bass used to say all the time?"

"'Bout?…Oh! Said he didn't believe in coincidences."

"Nor do I," Winchester concurred, as Boy tuned up again somewhere outside above the falls.

This time Son joined in…

WEST ANADARCHE CREEK
CHICKASAW NATION

"You hear what that old doc said was in that satchel?" Chaney looked at Wheeler, and then took a sip of the fragrant stout trail brew from his tin cup. "'Member that marshal said he'd been down to Gainesville."

"You don't suppose he was part of the group that went out an' brought the bodies of them kids in that wuz in the paper, do ya?" The leader of the group spat a long stream of tobacco juice into the fire, making a log pop and sizzle.

There were five men about the washtub-sized campfire. Parsons was snoring loudly near the edge of the camp under a tree after taking more than a healthy dose of the Laudanum Doctor Ashalatubbi had given him for the pain.

Besides Chaney, Wheeler and Siterly, the other two were Rube Monohan and a bull of a man named Rizzo Mulligan—they were run of the mill gunslicks.

Wheeler glanced up at the gibbous moon above the trees to the west of their camp on Anadarche Creek. "Chaney, what say you and Mulligan slip into town. By the time you git there, the moon will have set and should be good an' dark...Bust into that redhide doctor's buildin' an' git that carpet bag he tol' his nurse to put in his office...Who knows, meby ol' lady luck has finally done turned our way."

ARDMORE
CHICKASAW NATION

Chaney and Rizzo pulled rein in front of the Blue Bell Cafe and tied up at the hitching rail—the restaurant was closed for the evening. There were single gas street lights at the corner of each block. They looked up and down Carter Street—the town was quiet.

Doctor Ashalatubbi's office was a little over two hundred feet to the north of the cafe, in the center of the block.

The two men slipped between the Blue Bell and Clara's Millenary next door and headed to the alley behind the street front businesses.

"Dang, cain't hardly see my hand in front of my face," said Mulligan as they shuffled down the alleyway toward the doctor's office.

"Ow, you damn big ox. Quit steppin' on me...Move over thataway...Yer as wide as two ax handles." Chaney shoved on the big man's shoulder.

"What if'n I run into somethin'?"

"Jest don't knock it down an' make a bunch of racket."

"How're we gonna know when we git there?"

"Rizzo, did yer mama have any kids that lived?"

"Why, shore...I got a brother...But, what does that have to do with us findin' the doc's place?"

Mulligan couldn't see Chaney glaring his way in the dark.

"If brains was dynamite, Rizzo, you couldn't blow yer nose...I'm countin' my steps. When I git to the right number, that'll be it."

"Huh? How kin you count in the dark...I cain't even see my fangers."

"Oh, Jesus...Never mind...Think this is it."

"If'n you say so."

Chaney felt around for the back door. "Here, knock this door in." He put Rizzo's hand on the doorknob.

The big man grabbed the brass knob and lunged with his more than ample bulk at the six paneled back entrance. There was a splintering of the jam and the flimsy door sprung open.

"By the Lord Harry, it's even darker in there than it is out here...if that's possible," said Rizzo as he stood in the destroyed doorway.

"That's why God created matches."

"God created matches?...I didn't know that."

Chaney shouldered his way past the behemoth, reached in his vest pocket, pulled out a strike-anywhere Lucifer and popped his thumbnail over the head. The match hissed and flared with a sulfur smell, its yellow glow illuminating the room. "Uh, oh."

"What?"

"You busted in the wrong door. This is the tobacco shop just past the doctor's office."

"Well, I jest..."

"Shut up an' git outta my way...You big lummox." He grabbed a box of cigars off a shelf on the way out.

Rizzo turned, stepped back into the alleyway and waited on Chaney to lead. The gunslinger stomped out and over to the next building in the direction of the cafe.

He found the door, they repeated the process and Chaney lit another match.

"Awright, this is it."

He moved down a hall past the treatment room to Winchester's office, and then struck another match when the first one got too close to his fingers.

They looked around, Chaney opened a camel-back trunk that was against the wall and dumped it upside down. Rizzo turned Ashalatubbi's mahogany desk over—nothing.

Chaney lit another match. "Look in that metal cabinet in the corner."

Rizzo jerked open the double doors—nothing but supplies were inside. He slung it to the middle of the room in frustration. "Dammit!"

"The old bastard must have taken it with him," said Chaney. He turned, headed to the door. "We're pissin' up a rope...Let's get the hell outta here." He paused. "Make it look like a tornado came through here first."

ARDMORE
CHICKASAW NATION

It was almost ten in the morning when Jack pulled the mules to a halt in front of Doctor Ashalatubbi's clinic. "Ho up there, boys."

After setting the brake, he wrapped the ribbons around the hand lever and stepped down. Jack walked to the front of the team and tied their lead to an iron ring in the curb while Winchester was stepping down with his medical valise and the carpet bag.

"Reckon Abigail has some coffee on?" asked Jack.

"She usually does, come on in. Thought you had to take the mules over to the smithy's for some new shoes?"

"Do. But, hadn't had no coffee since we left the house 'fore daybreak."

Winchester grinned. "Well, God forbid you go mor'n four hours without a cup of coffee."

They walked to the front door and Winchester opened it. His nurse was sitting in one of the wooden chairs in the waiting room—the only one upright. Her face was buried in her hands and she was sobbing. A quick glance of the room told the men why. There were a couple of confused tribal patients standing behind her.

"Abigail, are you all right?" Winchester stepped over, set his bags on the floor, helped her to her feet and hugged the young woman. "*Foshi Lakna chinchokma*? Are you all right, Yellow Bird?" he repeated.

The young Chickasaw maiden looked up into his kindly face, shook her head and muttered, "*Akthano, Anompoli Lawa*." She repeated in English, "I do not know, He Who Talks to Many."

Yellow Bird wiped the tears from her cheeks. "I found the office this way when I opened up this morning...Why would someone do something like this?" She glanced around at the destruction.

"My office too?"

She nodded. "Everything."

Jack and Winchester exchanged glances.

"Well, I think this answers our question about coincidences, Uncle."

"It does, Jack, it does indeed." He looked at the carpet bag by his right foot. "We need to go send a telegram."

"Figured as much."

"You go ahead, Doctor, I'll get started straightening this mess up." Yellow Bird looked around again at the devastation and took a deep breath.

Winchester turned to the two patients. "Can you come back in an hour or so?"

The man and woman both nodded.

The Chickasaw glanced at his wife and smiled. *"Okti' Tohbi im eho puskush sapila."*

"Akostinichili. Chokmáshki...I understand. Thank you." He looked at Jack. "Ready?"

"Anytime."

They headed out the door.

"My Chickasaw ain't too sharp. What'd he say?" Jack asked as he untied the mules.

"He said he thinks his wife, White Snow, is with child."

"Ah…They say that's goin' 'round…Reckon he knows what caused it?"

"I'd say he's got a fair idea."

SKEANS BOARDING HOUSE
GAINESVILLE, TEXAS

Faye let the new deputy sheriff in the front door.

"Got a telegram fer Deputy F.M. Miller," he said.

"In here," Fiona said from the parlor.

The sandy-headed young man snatched his pinch-crowned brown hat from his head as he walked into the room. "Yer F.M. Miller?"

"So they tell me." She held out her hand.

"Sorry, Ma'am, wadn't 'spectin' a woman…The sheriff didn't happen to mention it…He just said…"

"Heard that before and don't call me, Ma'am…Deputy will do fine."

He handed her the yellow flimsy.

"Yessum, uh…Deputy." He nervously twisted his hat around in his hands and glanced at both Bill and Jim.

"What do they call you, Deputy?…I mean, what's your name?"

"Uh, my name is Jasper Argyle Wasson, but my momma calls me Buster, uh, Wasson."

"Your momma calls you Buster Wasson?"

"Well, if'n she's mad at me, she calls me Jasper Argyle, but mostly just Buster…that is."

She shook her head, unfolded it, read the missive and looked over at Bill, and then Jim. "Well, well, this is interesting."

Fiona turned to the young deputy who was holding a small spiral note pad and a short yellow pencil. "Take this down. Headed your way, next available train…Stop…Fiona…Stop." She handed him a Morgan silver dollar.

He looked at the coin in his hand and handed it back. "Oh, no, Ma'am, uh, Deputy. Cain't take this…part of the job. Walt, uh, the sheriff'll have my hide…but I'll see this gets right out."

The twenty-two year old law officer spun on his heel and headed out the front, letting the screen door slam.

Faye winced. "I hate it when they do that."

"Well?" asked Bill, looking at Fiona.

"It seems those yahoos who shot Jim and killed Walt's Deputy Muller headed off to the Nations, like we thought. Jack ran across them up above Turner Falls…One of them had fallen in a sinkhole, broken an arm and a leg. He sent them to Doctor Ashalatubbi's in Ardmore…They apparently got there about the same time as Jack and Winchester."

"How did they know it was same bunch?" asked Bill.

"Well, that's the interesting part. They heard *Anompoli Lawa* tell his nurse to put some special Indian artifacts he brought with him in his office while he set the man's broken bones…Winchester's office was ransacked last night."

"Did they get the artifacts?" asked Jim as he pushed himself to his feet with a hickory cane.

"No. The Doc took them with him when they went back out to Jack's house."

"Five'll get you ten they were scouting for caves in the Arbuckles, just like they were at the Bar M…I'd say," said Bill.

"Winchester said there was more, but didn't want to put it in a telegram."

"Dog-gone-it! Doc Wellman said I had to stay off a horse at least until the stitches were removed," Jim exclaimed.

"How's it feeling, Hon?" asked Fiona.

"Well, really not all that bad, considerin'…It's just a tad sore."

She looked at Bill and then back to him. "If you think you can handle riding in a buckboard, you and Ruth Ann could go…At least we can have some time together…I'm so sorry all of this has come up, but that's the nature of being a peace officer."

"I'm not real long on masochism, but I think I can handle it."

"But, you'll have to promise to stay at Jack and Angie's. They have a little girl, Baby Sarah…She's almost two."

"Ruthie will eat that up. Never seen anyone that loves babies mor'n her."

"Promise me you'll stay at the house?" She raised her eyebrows.

"All right, all right, I'll stay at the house…Ma'am." He grinned at her.

"What about me?" asked Bodie.

Annabel cleared her throat and glared at him.

He flashed his Cheshire cat grin at her and turned back to Fiona. "Well?"

"One, you have to get Doctor Wellman's clearance and two, you realize you don't have any jurisdiction up there."

"Huh…Well, neither do you." He got to his feet and headed to the door.

"Where are you going?" asked Annabel.

"Gonna walk over to Doc Wellman's and git him to write me out a permission slip." He stopped, cocked his head and grinned again. "Just like in prep school."

BLUE WATER WOMAN

TRAIN DEPOT
ARDMORE, IT

The straight-stack 4x4x2 coal-fired locomotive released pressure from her boilers as soon as she stopped at the platform. Huge clouds of steam hissed out from each side causing the waiting passengers to back away and turn their faces until the steam dissipated.

Fiona stepped down the stairs, holding Ruth Ann's hand. She was followed by Bill, and then Bodie assisting Jim down the steps. They looked about and spotted Jack and Winchester coming around the corner of the depot building headed their way.

Jack and Bodie exchanged bear hugs.

"Good to see you, Uncle Jack."

"You too, slick. Glad to see yer finally up and around."

Ruth Ann looked up at Bodie. "I didn't know he was your uncle."

"He's not really…he's my godfather. He an' my daddy were in Lincoln's war together."

"Oh…What's Lincoln's war?"

"Some folks call it the War Between the States," said Winchester.

"Like the Civil War?"

"That too," said her father.

Fiona introduced Jim and Ruth Ann.

Jack shook the cavalry officer's hand, and then bent over to take his daughter's. "And how are you, little lady?"

She curtsied and replied, "I'm fine, sir, and you?"

He gave her a big toothy smile and took her small bag. "If I were any better, sweetheart, I couldn't stand my own self."

Ruthie cocked her head for a moment, and then grinned. "Oh!"

"Jack doesn't always speak the Queen's English, Ruthie," said Winchester.

She put her hands on her hips. "I understood him just fine, Doctor Ashalatubbi...Thank you."

ARBUCKLE MOUNTAINS

Jack reined the mules off the main wagon road north to the smaller road leading west down into Honey Creek valley where his and Angie's home was located.

Jim rode on the seat next to him while Doctor Ashalatubbi and Ruth Ann were in the back of the wagon sitting on a couple of bales of oat straw.

Their baggage was stacked in the center along with a couple of apple boxes of supplies they had picked up at Jolley's General Store on the way from Ardmore.

Bill, Fiona and Bodie walked their mounts just behind the wagon.

"It's shame Walt couldn't come," said Doctor Ashalatubbi.

"He said he had to meet with the mayor again. Seems the city is adding a police department and they want Walt to train the chief and the first group," commented Fiona.

"Well, that would have made three of us without jurisdiction, anyhoo" said Bodie.

"I have the power to appoint possemen, but the problem is, don't have 'ny paper on anyone," added Jack. "We kin always go down to Ardmore an' fetch Selden an' Loss, if need be."

"Oh, look," said Ruth Ann. "A white doggie."

Jack turned slightly toward her. "That's Son, he's a wolf-dog. Always knows when I'm a comin' an' meets me here in the road." He chuckled. "The scudder will turn in a moment an' scoot down to the house to let Angie know we're almost there, and then he'll come back an' lead us in."

"He can talk?" she asked.

"Well, same as," Jack said as Son barked once, spun a circle in the road twice and sprinted away around a bend up ahead.

"See, he's headin' to the house."

"There's another one." Ruth Ann looked up at Jack. "Do you have two?" She pointed to a large white shape running alongside the road, ten yards up in the woods to their right, keeping pace with the wagon.

"See Uncle, there's Boy. Told you I seen him."

"Do believe you're right, Jack."

"And there's two more. Look there." Ruthie pointed higher up the side of the valley at two more white shapes running side-by-side through the woods, parallel to the wagon road.

Fiona, Bill and Bodie exchanged glances, and then looked at *Anompoli Lawa.*

The Chickasaw Shaman raised his hand to them and nodded. "I believe we're all right."

Ruth Ann turned to him. "What do you mean, Doctor?"

"Ruthie, you remember when we were sanctifying the pearls in Faye's back yard?"

She nodded.

"And the eagle that was watching us from the top of that big pine tree next to the carriage house flew off and I said he was one of *Chí-hóo-wah's* Guardians?"

She watched as the big animals disappeared in the brush. "Oh, are those white wolves Guardians, too?"

"They are that, child, they certainly are that."

"Are they mean?"

"I hope they are…to everybody but us."

MCGANN HOME
ARBUCKLE MOUNTAINS

Jack turned the mules into the paddock next to the barn along with Bill, Bodie and Fiona's mounts and followed the others to the house.

Angie was still hugging everybody as he climbed the steps to the front porch. Baby Sarah took Ruth Ann's hand and led her inside.

"Well, it's glad I am I fried up two pullets an' made a peach cobbler instead of a pie."

"Do you need some help finishing supper, Angie?" asked Fiona.

"I do indeed, sweet lady. The potatoes are ready for the smashin' while I make up some sawmill gravy…if ye would."

"Don't suppose there's 'ny coffee on, is there, woman of the house?"

Angie put her hands on her shapely hips. "An' when have ye seen me stove when there wasn't a pot of the Arbuckle on, husband?"

"Jest askin', m'love."

"An' while ye be restin', ye can bring in some more wood. Me box by the stove is near empty."

"Yessum."

"An' ye can be gettin' some cups down for our guests. I'm thinkin' they'd like some coffee too…Fiona an' I are gonna be finishing up the supper."

WEST ANADARCHE CREEK
CHICKASAW NATION

Wheeler poured himself a cup of the stout trail brew from the tin pot that had been sitting on a flat rock next to the fire.

He looked over at Parsons, nodding under a large sycamore tree at the edge of camp. "Anson…wake up."

The tall, skinny-as-a-rail man blinked his eyes a couple of times, and then focused on Wheeler. "Huh?"

"…Kin you sit a horse?"

He wrinkled his forehead in a frown. "Don't know…Damn shore cain't git on one by myself," the pockmarked-faced man mumbled, took a pull from the small green pharmaceutical bottle containing Laudanum that Doctor Ashalatubbi had given him and put the cork stopper back in it.

"Well, you need to git yer ass back down to Dexter. We ain't got the time to look out fer ya."

"I don't see any way in hell I kin ride all the way down to Delaware Bend…Take eight er nine hours, I 'spect. Somebody's either gotta go with me er…"

BLUE WATER WOMAN

There was a roar of a .45 being discharged and a hole the size of a dime appeared in the middle of Parson's forehead. The man's eyes went wide as a narrow trickle of blood came out of the perfectly round hole and ran down the side of his nose. His eyes clicked back in his head and he slumped against the tree trunk, staring unseeing at the campfire.

Wheeler, Posey, Rube Monohan and Rizzo Mulligan all turned at the same time to look at Chaney. A large cloud of acrid black powder gunsmoke hung in the still air in front of him as the gunslick rotated his swivel holster back to the vertical position.

"Solves that problem, don't it?" he said as he blew across the top of his cup, licked the rim and took a sip.

Wheeler looked at him stoically, and then said, "Damnation, Chaney."

The gunfighter bit the end off one of the stolen cigars, spit it out and looked up. "What?"

Wheeler shook his head. "Nothin'." He took a deep breath and sat down on a nearby log. "Awright, here's the way it is. Boss man's convinced they's some of that Injun treasure he heered 'bout up here in the Arbuckles, if'n it ain't down 'long the river…So, here's what we're gonna do."

§§§

CHAPTER SEVEN

MCGANN HOME
ARBUCKLE MOUNTAINS

Angie had placed pallets out on the screened-in back porch for Bodie, Bill and Doctor Ashalatubbi. She fixed the daybed out there for Captain Bryan—Fiona and Ruth Ann got the spare bedroom next to Baby Sarah's.

Winchester, Fiona and Jack sat in the rockers, sipping on cups of hot coffee. Bodie and Bill were also having some, but were reclining against the side wall of the house on their pallets.

Angie was inside reading to the girls from *Alice's Adventures in Wonderland*.

"Aren't you going to lie down, Doc?" asked Jack.

"After I finish my coffee. Once I lay down on the floor, I fear I'll be there until morning...When you get to be my age, you'll understand that."

Bill chuckled. "Think I'm getting there already. This floor is just a step above the ground...but, not near as cold and there's no rocks."

"Jest glad it ain't wintertime er everbody would be bunched up like a pack of blue-tick hounds, layin' 'round the fireplace...It gits fair cold up here in the mountains," commented Jack.

"What's the plan of the mornin'?" asked Bill.

"Gonna go up to Crazy Mary's an' see if'n them miscreants knowed somethin', er wuz just scoutin' 'round," said Jack.

"What about that wild lady?" inquired Fiona. "You indicated she doesn't like strangers around."

Jack glanced at her. "That's why we stopped at Jolley's General Store on the way out. Knowd she likes snuff, so I got her a couple of the large six ounce glasses of Garrett's...Gonna give her a ham an' some sausage from the smokehouse, too."

"What is that quote?...'Beware of Greeks bearing gifts...or something like that, it was," said Bill with a grin.

"It's from The *Aeneid of Vergil*, referencing Odysseus leaving the Trojan Horse at the gates of Troy," said Fiona.

"Yeah, but we ain't Greek," offered Bodie.

"It's probably the prudent thing to do," said Winchester.

"Euripides said, 'Life has no blessing like a prudent friend'," added Fiona.

"I jest sometimes think all that crazy woman needs is a friend. That's why I take her things I know she would like, ever now an' then…At least it keeps her from chunkin' rocks at me when I go by huntin'," said Jack, smiling.

"You plan on going in her cave?" asked Bill.

"No need. Judgin' from what the Posey feller said when I pulled him outta that sinkhole…It's my thinkin' that the Honey actually starts further to the west, goes underground, an' then comes out past Wild Woman Cave…Goes down the mountain from there an' over the falls…"

Anompoli Lawa chuckled. "And Jack has personal experience with that. Fact is, we gave him a Chickasaw name…*Oka'-bia-Lawa*, He Who Talks With Water."

"I do."

"What do you mean…personal experience?" asked Fiona.

Winchester took a sip of his coffee. "Near two years ago, Jack and Chickasaw Lighthorse, Montford Anoatubbi, were working undercover here in the Arbuckles…going after claim jumpers. We had a small gold rush in the area and this jake-leg barrister in Ardmore, Jason Alexander Baldwin, hired a bunch of ne'er–do–well outlaws to jump claims…anyway they could…"

Jack joined in, "Montford an' me were lookin' fer a place to start placer minin' up near the headwaters of the Honey one mornin' right after a five-inch rain…Creek was on a real tear, I'm here to say…Well, we got ambushed. Kilt Montford right off. I took a ball in the side, an' then one bounced off'n my head…"

"Good thing they hit your head, Uncle Jack…or it mighta hurtcha," said Bodie with a grin.

He looked at his godson out of the corner of his eye. "If'n you break your leg, Bodie Hickman, don'tchu come a running to me."

They both laughed.

"Anyhoo, I fell into the white water an' it washed me down the mountain an' over them seventy-seven foot falls…Jest barely missed hittin' that big boulder in the middle of the pool at the bottom…Hellova ride, don'tcha know." Jack paused and looked at his cup for a moment. "Well, managed to crawl up in that cave behind the falls…" He shook his head. "Felt like I'd been chewed up, spit out, an' stepped on."

"That's when that little spirit girl found you?" asked Bodie.

Jack nodded. "Yep, sometime after Boy come in an' laid down next to me to keep me warm…Kept me from dying, he did…"

"Spirit girl? You mean a ghost?" asked Jim.

"Didn't know it at the time, but, that's what she was an' you kin hang yer hat on that…Talked to her jest like I'm talkin' to you now…pretty little blond-headed thing. Found out later that she wuz Angie's nine year old daughter what got washed over the falls, too…couple years earlier. They never had found her body then…but that's another story."

"This entire area is very spiritual and sacred to our people," said Ashalatubbi. "There are prehistoric petroglyphs in that cave Jack was in…One in particular that strongly resembles the Minorah."

"The ancient Hebrew solid gold lampstand that Moses had in the wilderness…and 300 years later was used in the Temple in Jerusalem?" questioned Fiona as she continued giving her long dark hair a nightly brushing.

Winchester nodded. "Yes, it had a distinctive shape and seven lamps, fueled by consecrated fresh olive oil."

"How can there be a prehistoric rock carving of the Minorah here in America? The white man didn't come to this area until the 1500s…The legend of the Minorah is over five thousand years old," she exclaimed.

BLUE WATER WOMAN

There was a twinkle in *Anompoli Lawa's* eyes. "Exactly, my dear...It's also associated with the Jewish holiday of Hanukkah...According to the Talmud, after the desecration of the Jewish Temple in Jerusalem by the Seleucid Empire, there was only enough sanctified olive oil left to fuel the flame from the Minorah in the Temple for one day...By some miracle, the oil lasted for eight days, allowing them time to make and consecrate new pure oil...giving rise to the Hebrew celebration of Eight Days of Hanukkah, their Winter Holidays."

"That's absolutely amazing," said Fiona.

"In addition, there are several hieroglyphs I recognized as being in the Masoretic Text...They illustrate....*Jehovah - God of Isreal.*"

Everyone on the porch leaned toward the Shaman in rapt attention.

"In the Muscogean language, which is shared by the Chickasaw, Choctaw and Creek...one of our words for the Great Spirit, or God, if you will, is...*Chí-hóo-wah.* I believe you can hear the close similarity."

There were several audible intakes of breath around the porch.

Bill shook his head in wonder. "So much for Columbus, I'd say."

"In reality, Marshal Roberts, he's a Johnny-come-lately to these shores." *Anompoli Lawa* looked around at the others. "…So you see why this is a holy place to us…We all worship the same God."

"Is there goin' to be a quiz on this, Doctor Ashalatubbi?" asked Bodie.

"Well, that's a capital idea, son. A capital idea." He grinned. "I can explain it all to you…but I can't understand it for you."

"Huh?"

"See?"

"I want to hear the story about the little ghost girl, Winchester…At nine, she was the same age as my Ruth Ann is now," said Jim.

Doctor Ashalatubbi glanced over at the young officer and nodded. "Her name was Anna…But, maybe later, Jim. Rather Angie be present to tell it. She and Jack were there…I never actually saw her. The spirits select only a precious few to show themselves to…I sensed her, though."

Jim laid back on the daybed, his hands clasped behind his head. "My, my, my, a revelation indeed."

BLUE WATER WOMAN

GAINESVILLE, TEXAS

The four gunmen sat their horses next to the black Stanhope buggy and listened to their instructions. The man inside, snipped the end of his Cuban cigar with an engraved silver cigar cutter that had once belonged to his deceased brother, Jason. Pocketing the keepsake, he took out a match, struck it on the canopy support to his right and twirled the expensive cigar around, warming the end and finally lighting it. He took a deep draw and blew a cloud of the fragrant smoke out the side of the buggy.

"Olinger, you find Wheeler and his bunch. They'll be camped alongside Caddo Creek, just east of Elk and north of Ardmore, according to his telegram. Tell him I said you're takin' over...Got that? We're going to kill two birds with one stone.

"There's only that woman, a deputy marshal and a Texas Ranger who's still a little on the mend from a gunshot, from here...and that deputy marshal that lives up there, Jack McGann. He'll be your huckleberry...Should be enough of you to take care of everything and get them out of the way."

"That ranger turned county sheriff didn't go?"

"No, he's busy with local politics...besides, it's out of his jurisdiction."

"Who's the other marshal?"

"Name's Brushy Bill Roberts...Nobody to worry about."

"And the woman?"

He chuckled. "You just answered your own question...she's a woman. Enough said."

Olinger nodded and smirked. "We'll leave first thing in the mornin'..."

"You'll leave right now." His dark eyes snapped at the man. "I want you there by sunup...Clear?"

"Uh...yes, sir."

"You have your instructions...Do not fail me." There was a touch of steel in his voice that removed any question John Olinger might have had.

MCGANN HOME
ARBUCKLE MOUNTAINS

Jack and Angie's Rhode Island Red rooster's morning call awakened everyone on the screened-in porch.

Bill rolled over in his blankets, raised up on an elbow and squinted at the big dark red bird with black tail feathers, perched on the top rail of the paddock by the barn. He watched him stretch and fluff his wings several times, face the pink horizon to the east and serenade the sunrise once more. "Well, no sleepin' with that goin' on."

He sat up, rubbed the sleep from his eyes and looked around at the others glancing angrily outside at the big bird.

"He probably thinks the sun comes up just to hear him crow," said Bodie as he smacked his lips, and then sniffed the air.

He looked over at the open doorway into the house. "I smell coffee." He threw his blanket off, reached for his boots and gave them a shake in case any scorpions or spiders had taken up residence during the night.

Bill was already up, stamping his feet down into his scalloped-top boots. "Is there anything in the world that smells better than coffee brewin' early in the morning?"

"I'd say bacon sizzlin' in the pan will run a close second," added Jim as he reached for his hickory cane.

Doctor Ashalatubbi helped himself to his feet by holding on to one of the chairs and grunting.

"Dang, Doc, does the moanin' an' groanin' help?" asked Bodie.

"Does when you get to be my age, you young pup." He stepped over to the screen door leading outside and pushed it open.

"Where you goin', coffee's this way," said Bodie as he walked to the door that opened to the kitchen.

"I'm goin' to go hug a rose bush, if it's all the same to you."

"Hug a rose bu…Oh! Right. I follow you."

"Rather you didn't," the elderly Chickasaw said over his shoulder as he headed toward the outhouse near the barn.

Bill looked at the young ranger, grinned and followed him into the kitchen.

"Well, it's about time, it is, ye be risin'…Was thinkin' ye were goin' to be sleepin' half the day away," said Angie as she stirred the big bowl of pancake batter at the counter.

"Smelled the coffee," said Roberts.

Fiona was at Angie's wood-burning stove, turning the bacon in a big cast iron skillet with a fork. "Bill always needs a stimulus to get started of the morning." She picked up a hot pad and grabbed the half-gallon light-blue speckled graniteware pot from the stove.

He procured a white porcelain mug from the cabinet and held it out for her to fill. "No, it's just that you make better coffee than I do, m'lady."

"Uh, huh. A convenient thing to say when I'm holding the pot, Marshal." She filled Jim and Bodie's cups also before setting the pot back on the stove. "Where's Doctor Ashalatubbi?"

"He said he was goin' out to…"

"You don't have to tell everything you know, Bodie," said Winchester as he came through the door followed by Jack.

Fiona filled two more cups for the late arrivals.

Doctor Ashalatubbi turned around, somewhat startled. "Jack! Didn't know you were behind me. Quiet as you were, you could be Indian."

"I am quarter Potawatomi, you know, Uncle...I was feedin' the stock while ya'll were still cuttin' logs." He took his mug from Fiona. "Much obliged."

"If ye'll be takin' yer seats at the table, I'll be bringin' the breakfast out."

"Wow, that's fair quick, Angie," said Bodie.

"My bride's special, she is. She can get there in half less than no time," said Jack.

"Do what?" asked Bodie.

"He means there's no slack in her rope," said Winchester.

Hickman shook his head. "Why didn't you just say so instead of goin' by way of Melviney?"

Jack looked at his godson over the top of his cup. "Did."

"They do this all the time?" Jim asked Doctor Ashalatubbi.

He nodded. "Pretty much."

"I'm glad they like each other so well," said Fiona.

"Have to, we're related...sort of," commented Jack as he stepped through the door to the dining room and sat down at the head of the long oak table.

The rest pulled out chairs and took seats also. The mouthwatering aroma of bacon, sausage and pancakes with warmed sorghum syrup filled the room as Angie and Fiona started bringing the steaming platters from the kitchen.

CADDO CREEK
CHICKASAW NATION

The big barrel-chested, John Olinger and his three men, Mo Brown, Big Jim Allison and Dudley Mabry, rode into the camp by the creek and dismounted.

"What're ya'll doin' here Olinger?" asked Wheeler as he got to his feet.

"Bossman sent us. I'm takin' over." He removed his green bowler, wiped his forehead with a calico kerchief, and then set it back on his balding head.

"The hell you say."

"Ain't open for discussion. You know how he is when he gives an order."

Wheeler looked over at Chaney, and then back to Olinger. "Awright...What the hell. Gittin' paid the same either which-a-way...We wuz jest fixin' to ride up to the mountains and start goin' through them caves near the crazy woman's...Jest finishin' our coffee."

"No...You, Posey and Rizzo are goin' to that marshal's house. Kill him...if he's there."

"An' if'n he's not?"

"Grab his wife…Hold her till he shows up."

"Then what?"

"Kill 'em both…They're responsible for the Boss' brother gettin' hung by Parker."

Wheeler nodded. "Hear tell they got a little kid."

"So?"

"What do you want me to do…"

"Want me to draw you a picture, dunderhead?…What do you think?"

"Right…What er ya'll gonna be doin'?"

"We'll be up goin' through them caves like you shoulda already done."

"Well, wadn't our fault…Parsons got his self all busted up. Had to take 'im to see that Injun doctor."

Olinger looked around the camp. "Where is he now?"

Wheeler glanced at Chaney again. "Uh, he didn't make it…Buried him back over yonder in the woods." He pointed with his head.

"Just as well…Put that fire out and saddle up. The boss don't cotton to the way you been gettin' caught in your own loop, so see to it you change your ways." Olinger glared at him for a moment. "You don't want me to have to say it again, Wheeler." He stuck his foot in the oxbow stirrup and swung into the saddle. "Chaney, you and Rube with me…Let's ride."

MCGANN HOME
ARBUCKLE MOUNTAINS

After breakfast, Fiona changed from her split riding skirt to her light tan buckskins and knee-length Apache-style moccasins she always wore when she went out on the trail. She slipped her ten-inch, bone-handled, Bowie knife under her gunbelt in the middle of her back. Her long raven hair was in a thick single braid and draped over her left shoulder.

"Hey, those are nice buckskins."

"Not really buckskins, Bodie...doeskins. Much softer and lighter. My late husband's Cherokee grandmother made them for me."

"Love to have a set."

"I've been trying to find someone to make me some too, Bodie," offered Bill.

"Just happen to know some Chickasaw ladies over at Ada that can take care of that for you gentlemen. They just need your measurements," commented Winchester.

"Awright, everybody out to the barn. Got some stuff we gotta make up," said Jack.

Thirty minutes later, out in the barn, they had made a half-dozen torches out of inch-thick, three foot long willow sticks with numerous strips of old burlap wrapped around one end and tied with bailing wire. Each torch was drenched in coal oil, and then coated with roof pitch made from pine tree sap.

"These should last a good two hours each once we light 'em," commented Jack. "The smoke should also scare away the spiders down there."

"There's spiders in the caves?" asked Bodie.

"Like stars in the sky around the entrances, like stars in the sky…They're just granddaddy long legs, though, ain't gonna hurtcha none."

Bodie shook like a wet mule. "Don't care…Hate spiders. Don't want 'em crawlin' on me."

"Good, you get to carry the torches, slick nickel."

"Gotta learn to keep my mouth shut."

Jack looked at him while he bagged up Crazy Mary's supplies in a flour sack. "Been tellin' you that since you wuz a kid…Yer jest a bit slow on the uptake."

"Aw, Uncle Jack…am not."

Fiona shook her head and grinned as she tightened Spot's front cinch, forked her saddle and joined Brushy Bill, Bodie and Winchester already mounted. Jack stepped up on Chief and led the group out.

Angie and Jim waved at them from the porch as they rode out of the yard toward the falls. Ruth Ann and Baby Sarah had just gotten up, were holding hands, and waved too.

HONEY CREEK

The group rode single file along the game trail that paralleled the clear mountain creek. Jack still led the way with Son running alongside, occasionally stopping to smell some coon scat or mark a bush.

Fiona glanced over at Bill. "You've changed pistols, partner…That's a Colt Single Action Frontier. What happened to your Thunderer?"

He opened his coat to show the bird's head double-action Colt in a shoulder holster. "Decided to go back to my favorite, a .44-40 single action. Was practicin' with the Thunderer and the hammer jammed on me…Not designed for fast trigger action. It's my backup now."

"Didn't want to say anything, but that happened to me once when I was picking which guns to carry. Double action is fine for target practicing, but not reliable when one's life is on the line."

"I'd say."

Several hundred yards after they passed the headwaters where the creek flowed out of a small cave in the side of a cliff, they approached Wild Woman Cave. They were met by banshee-like screeches and rocks being lobbed in front of them from behind some large boulders.

"Dang, that's like fingernails on a blackboard," commented Bodie as he scrunched his shoulders up.

Jack held up his hand for everybody behind him to stop and shouted, "Mary! Mary! It's Marshal McGann. Quit yer chunkin'. Got some things fer you."

A scratchy voice came back from behind the rocks. "Who's all them folks with you?"

"My godson, another marshal, a deputy sheriff and the Chickasaw Shaman, *Anompoli Lawa*."

"It's ol' Winchester, you've got with ye?"

"I do."

"Mary's seen him not since before the big war."

Jack looked back at Doctor Ashalatubbi and raised one eyebrow.

Winchester frowned, lifted his shoulders and shook his head.

They rode around the copse of dogwood Jack had hidden in earlier, and then up to the boulders. Mary stepped out holding a long walking staff.

"It's enough fer a chivaree, did you bring, Marshal?"

155

Jack and the others dismounted and he untied the flour sack from his saddlehorn. "Brought you some things, Mary."

She snatched the bag from his hand, and then looked around behind him. "It's changed much you haven't Winchester Ashalatubbi, exceptin' fer the fat. It's big enough to butcher fer lard you are."

He frowned again and looked at the old woman trying to figure out if he knew her. "I'm sorry, madam, but, do I know you?"

She cackled and spat a stream of brown watery snuff juice to the side. "Sparkin' me you did, you old coot…It's kids in school we were."

His eyes went wide as saucers. "Mary Louise? Mary Louise Waters?"

She looked off for a moment, pensively, and then back to him. "A coon's age it's been since Mary's heered her whole name." She nodded. "Mary I am…Pert as a cricket, she thought always you were, but puttin' socks on a rooster be easier than gettin' Winchester to dance…It's different directions yer two left feet wanted to take." She cackled again, and then opened the sack and looked inside.

Winchester blushed. "Mary Louise Waters." He shook his head.

She pulled out one of the large glass jars of snuff. "It's blessin' you I am, Marshal…an' a ham too. Christmas you must believe." Mary slipped the snuff in a large rabbit-skin pouch she had hung around her neck. "But, it's not in Mary's place you'll be thinkin' of goin'. Rights you don't have." She nodded, turned and disappeared back into her cave.

"Well, that worked...Let's head thataway." He pointed to the southwest, and then glanced at Winchester. "You too...Uncle Twinkle Toes."

The venerable Chickasaw physician squinted his eyes. "Don't start with me, Jack...Dancing just was never high on my list."

"Uh, huh."

"How did she wind up here? Do you have any idea?" asked Fiona.

"Well, sometime shortly after Lincoln's war, it's my understanding she was married and had two toddlers...a boy and a girl. A group of red-leg renegades rode into their place, burned it to the ground, killed her husband, butchered her babies and took turns raping her for near a week. She completely disappeared after that. No one knew what came of her...until now. Guess it was too much for her mind to handle...Such a pity."

"I chased a renegade like that for two years who killed my husband."

"I'm assuming you're referring to the Cherokee, Calvin Mankiller," said Ashalatubbi. "The one that shot Bodie and kidnapped Faye."

"Among other things...Yes,I am. He was totally devoid of moral turpitude or scruples, a true sociopath...Killed men, women and children...raping, butchering and scalping. Age didn't seem to matter."

"I heard you caught up to him?"

Fiona looked at Doctor Ashalatubbi for a moment, but Bill interrupted before she could reply, "She did indeed. I was there. Introduced him to his first day in hell...piece at a time. Put nine shots in the evil bastard...the last one between his black eyes. All the while with Mankiller's Bowie stuck in her."

She took a deep breath. "I scarcely remember that day...I just knew I had to make him pay for his crimes...Couldn't count on some softhearted gutless judge administering his perverted interpretation of justice."

"You said something after the cavalry doc stitched you up...What was it? Oh, I remember...'In a nation that becomes too civilized to administer equal and exact justice to evil...barbarians will rule'."

§§§

CHAPTER EIGHT

HONEY MOUNTAIN

Jack and the group of riders, pulled rein a little over a quarter of a mile west of the entrance to Mary's cave. They loosened the girths and hobbled their mounts in a small swag next to a grove of persimmon trees.

"They's plenty of grass there to keep the boys occupied fer a spell…Everbody git yer lariats," said Jack.

They each undid their ropes from their saddles, slipped them over their head and one arm and followed Jack as he led them about fifty yards further west.

"Didn't know 'bout the little sinkhole that ne'er-do-well, Parsons, fell into back yonder closter to Mary's cave, but, knowed 'bout this one fer quite a spell. It's a sight bigger an' we kin climb down instead of havin' to be lowered."

"Then why are we taking the ropes?" Bill inquired.

"Never go underground without takin' a couple ropes along…Jest don't always know what yer gonna find down there."

"We all gonna go down, Uncle Jack?" asked Bodie.

"Nope, better leave a couple up topside…jest in case they's trouble." He turned to Winchester. "Doc, you best stay…An' how's Bodie's chest wound a healin'?"

"Aw, I'm fine as frog hair, Uncle Jack."

"Ain't askin' you, slick, I'm askin' the doctor. This is a medical decision." He turned back to Ashalatubbi again. "Well, Doc? Whatcha think?"

"Bodie doesn't need to be going down there. One, he's still healing and will be for the next four to five months." He looked at the young ranger. "That .44 caliber bullet shattered your breast bone, son, not to say anything about the soft tissue damage…Two, it's damp in those caves and your lungs can't handle prolonged dampness. You had a touch of pneumonia, you know…End of discussion."

"There you have it, sunshine. You and Winchester stay up here. Let me have yer rope."

Bodie frowned and nodded. "Awright…You're as bad as my Annabel." He slipped his lariat over his head and handed it to Jack.

"We're jest lookin' out fer you…on account of the bullheadedness you inherited from yer daddy…among other things. Leastwise you don't have to worry 'bout them spiders," Jack said as he put Bodie's rope over his head on top of his.

He grinned and nodded again. "Got a point there, Uncle Jack."

"Ya'll kin build a little fire and put some coffee on fer us when we come out." He looked at Bill and Fiona. "Jest as well leave yer hats up here too. Be 'bout as useless as hip pockets on a hog down there."

They set them on top of a granite boulder a few feet from the entrance.

Jack took the torches from Bodie and started down the large hole. The big wolf-dog started to follow him. "Son, you stay up here."

The animal whined, backed up, sat down next to Winchester and watched as his master disappeared into the earth. Jack was followed by Bill and Fiona.

THE CAVE

They climbed over the rubble and detritus from the surface that had been created when the limestone weakened and collapsed to the cave below. The loose dirt and rock formed a sort of ramp to the bottom.

Once on the semi-flat cave floor, Jack handed Fiona and Bill two torches each. "Now, we'll only light two at the time." He scratched a Lucifer on his gunbelt and lit one of the two he was carrying, and then one of Bill's.

The pitch covering the balls of burlap slowly caught fire and cast a flickering yellow glow on the cave walls. What they could see of the ceiling, varied from a little over five feet to nearly ten feet. The glow disappeared ahead like it was a living thing being swallowed up by the cimmerian darkness.

"Watch yer head, sometimes that roof kin dip down, er they's stone icicle things stickin' down…"

"Stalactites…The ones hanging from the ceiling are called stalactites…and those sticking up from the floor are stalagmites."

"How in Sam hell do they stick up from the floor?"

"They're both caused by drops of water from the ceiling carrying minerals. If you'll look, there's always a stalactite directly above a stalagmite. Eventually they can meet and form a column," said Fiona.

"Well, whatever…smarts like hell if'n you run in to one with yer head."

"I'd say," Bill commented.

"I'm sure there'll be other formations created by water…curtins, soda straws, bacon…"

"Bacon?" Jack blurted.

"It's another type of formation caused by water that looks like bacon in a skillet."

"Huh…Butter my butt an' call me a biscuit."

"I don't think so, I don't," said Bill.

"How far have you been up this cave, Jack?" asked Fiona.

He chuckled. "'Bout another fifty feet er so…Never had 'ny reason to go further before…I 'spect they's five to six miles of cave been cut through this here rock."

They rounded a turn and Jack came to a sudden stop. "What in…"

Just inside the glow from the torch was an odd shaped shiny four-foot high rock formation.

"Looky there," Jack said.

"Looks like three elephants standing side-by-side facing away from us," commented Fiona.

"You mean it looks like three elephant butts…It does," added Bill.

"I think I said that, Marshal."

The cave widened out into a cavern showing more and more water-created formations. The light bouncing from the glossy surfaces of the travertine reflected every color of the rainbow.

"Unbelievably beautiful…It's a fairy world wonderland," said Fiona under her breath. "Oh! Down there." She pointed. "Looks like someone threw a blanket against the wall…It's like the rock is actually flowing down the side."

"Listen, hear that?" said Jack.

"Water…rushing water," commented Bill.

MCGANN HOME

Ruth Ann, holding Baby Sarah's hand, walked into the kitchen where Angie was finishing cleaning up the breakfast things.

"Miz McGann, is it all right if I take Baby Sarah down along the creek for a walk and look for wild flowers?"

Angie froze for a moment recalling how her daughter, Anna, was searching for jonquils when she fell into the creek above the falls five long years ago. She took a deep breath to clear her mind. "I suppose so, Ruth Ann, but don't go near the creek. It's not running swift this time of year, but I still don't want you girls to get too close…Understand?"

"Yes, ma'am."

BLUE WATER WOMAN

They went out the front screen door, past Ruth Ann's father sitting in a rocker and reading one of Angie's new books, *The Red Badge of Courage* by Stephen Crane. He looked up as the girls went down the steps.

"Hey, just where do you young ladies think you're off to?"

"We're going flower hunting, daddy. Miz McGann said it was all right."

He frowned. "Well...don't go far and stay on the path."

"We won't and we will."

"Come again?"

Ruth Ann turned back to her father, put her hands on her hips and spoke slowly, "We *won't* go far and we *will* stay on the path." She nodded at him with one single bob of her head.

"Oh, right...Well, watch for snakes."

Ruthie grinned and waved at him as she and Baby Sarah ran toward the gate. She opened it and they headed to the trail through the woods that went all the way to the falls.

The girls strolled along the path a little over a hundred yards from the house. Ruth Ann was still holding Baby Sarah's hand, but each had a bunch of flowers in their other hand, including Indian Paintbrushes and some Baby Blue Eyes.

They stopped at a cluster of Purple Morning Glory that were still open.

"Oh, aren't these pretty, Baby Sarah?"

165

The toddler nodded vigorously and held out her hand. "Prettly."

They were startled by a deep voice. "Well, looky here, Wheeler, looky here. We got some little girls a pickin' flowers."

Ruth Ann stepped back, looked up at the giant of a man towering over them. A smaller, weasel-eyed man and a short stocky individual also stepped out from each side of a three-foot diameter cottonwood.

She hugged Baby Sarah close to her. "What do you want?

"Which one of youz is Marshal McGann's daughter?" asked the big one, Rizzo Mulligan.

"Why?" Ruthie answered.

"You got a smart mouth on you fer sech a little squirt of a thang," said the stocky man, Monte Wheeler. He spat a long stream of tobacco juice at the girl's feet.

"That's nasty," Ruth Ann said.

"Sez who?"

"I say."

"An' you are?"

"Ruth Ann Bryan, for your information."

Wheeler looked at Rizzo, and then Posey. "Well, answers that question, don't it, boys?...Come'ere missy." He reached for Baby Sarah's arm.

Ruth Ann twisted away and moved the little girl behind her. "No!"

"Now, we ain't gonna hurt her none. We jest need to keep her handy till her paw comes back. Seen him an' some others ride off this mornin' up the mountain…Figger they'll be back soon. So, git over here," commanded Wheeler.

Ruth Ann threw up her chin. "I said, no."

Rizzo stepped forward and raised his huge ham-like hand to strike her, but stopped instantly when a giant golden-eyed white wolf crept out of the woods behind the girls and growled low.

The big man staggered back. "Oh, sweet Jes…" Was all he got out before the beast launched itself through the air at his throat, taking him to the ground.

The animal mauled the giant of a man for a few seconds before tearing his throat out. Rizzo gurgled, thrashed about, shook one final time, and then died. The wolf spun around and took Posey down who was frozen in fear. He snapped his neck with one bite.

Wheeler took off running and screaming through the woods as the bloody-faced wolf turned and looked at Ruth Ann and Baby Sarah as they hugged each other.

"It's all right, Boy," said a soft child's voice.

The girls looked up as another young girl, in a red calico dress, about the same age as Ruth Ann, also with long blond curls and blue eyes, stepped out from behind the cottonwood.

"Who are you?" asked Ruth Ann.

"I'm Anna." She placed her arm across the big wolf's massive shoulders. "Boy and I came to help you against those bad men."

HONEY MOUNTAIN

Bodie had scrounged up enough deadfall to build a hat-sized fire. Winchester filled the pot with water from his canteen, threw in a couple of handfuls of ground Arbuckle and set it on a rock next to the blaze.

Doctor Ashalatubbi squatted down, pulled out his briarwood pipe, filled it from a leather pouch and reached for a burning twig at the edge of the fire. He held it over the bowl and drew a couple of puffs.

Son, lying next to his feet, suddenly snapped his head up, looked toward a ridge of rocks to the west and growled. Winchester and the big wolf-dog both got to their feet as six riders came around the edge of the boulders.

"You the Injun doctor?" asked Olinger as they reined their horses to a stop.

"I am. Don't think I know you sir." He looked at Chaney. "Recognize that one, though."

"Where's the rest of them?"

"Who?"

"Don't play games with me, old man." Olinger pointed at the hats on the boulder and drew his Colt.

The hair on the back of Son's neck rose up as a deep growl rumbled in his throat.

"It's that marshal's damn dog…Gonna kill it." Chaney rotated his holster and fired.

Son was a hair quicker as he dodged to the side and dove down the sink hole. Chaney drew the .44-40 from the holster, thumbed the hammer and fired again. The bullet ricocheted from the stone around the entrance and whined off in the distance.

"Dammit."

Down the hill a short distance, Bodie dropped the armload of deadfall he had gathered for the fire when he heard the shot. He loosened his Peacemaker in its holster and crept up to a copse of cedars that were between him and the campsite.

He peered through the thick green boughs covered with tiny purple berries at the six men on horseback facing Winchester.

"Don't do nothin' Doc," he whispered. "Don't do nothin'."

"I asked you a question, redhide. Ain't accustomed to askin' twict." He cocked the hammer on his Colt.

"Hey, Olinger, look," one of the gunhands, Big Jim Allison said and pointed.

There was a huge white wolf on top of a boulder less than a hundred feet away. His golden eyes seemed to stare right through the outlaws.

"There's another," said Mo Brown as he drew his Remington revolver.

"Neither one of them's the marshal's…They're way bigger. What in hell?" exclaimed Chaney.

"Another one over there," said Rube. "An' another," he yelled as he twisted in his saddle. "They're all 'round us."

The giant animals were slowly stalking toward the men, bellies almost brushing the ground—their lips were pulled back in a snarl showing long white canine teeth.

"I'm gittin' outta here," said Dudley as he wheeled his bay about and viciously dug his large rowel spurs into the hapless animal's ribs.

"Come back here, fool," shouted Olinger. "They're…"

He was interrupted by one of the animals springing from the top of a boulder, hitting Dudley Mabry in the chest and taking him to the ground. The panicked horse kicked his hind legs high in the air and bolted down the mountain, bucking all the way.

The giant wolf picked the man up by the throat and shook him like a dead rat. He dropped the body to the ground, placed one saucer-sized paw on his chest and ripped out his throat—blood spurted in all directions.

Chaney fired a shot at the beast, who turned, snarled at him and ducked back behind the boulder. "Jesus H. Christ…I know I hit him. No way I miss at this distance."

"Well, apparently you did." Olinger sneered, turned back to Winchester and calmly shot the old physician in the right foot.

Anompoli Lawa cried out in pain and fell to the ground, holding his bleeding appendage.

"That's fer not answerin' me, old man…Told you I didn't play games nor ask twice."

He wheeled his red roan gelding about and spurred him in the side. "Let's git outta here…We'll be back," he said.

Son poked his head out of the sinkhole as the outlaws rode out of sight. He trotted over and laid down beside the moaning Chickasaw Shaman.

Bodie ran up and dropped to his knees. "Winchester, how bad are you hurt?"

Anompoli Lawa raised up, made the sign of friend to the white wolves and said, "*Chi-hóo-wah-bia-chi*...Go with God, my friends."

The creatures faded into the brush.

Winchester turned his head back to Bodie. "Bastards shot me in the foot out of pure meanness. Help me get my boot off. Need to stop the bleeding."

The ranger picked up the old physician's leg, gently tugged his boot off and held it up for Winchester to see.

"Well, went all the way through." Bodie stuck his finger in the bullet hole in the bottom.

Ashalatubbi nodded. "Thank the Lord for small blessings...Now, fetch my bag from my horse."

"Be right back." He turned and sprinted back east to where the horses were picketed.

THE CAVE

The cave had widened into a cavern and increased in height even more to the point that the rushing creek occupied one side for almost thirty yards before it cut to the right and disappeared under an overhang ahead.

Jack stopped and turned to Fiona and Bill. "Did ya'll hear somethin'?"

"Like what?" asked Bill.

"Like a poppin' sound...a gunshot meby?"

They both shook their heads.

"I can't hear anything but that water," said Fiona.

Jack nervously glanced back up the darkened tunnel toward the entrance, and then headed on down the cavern.

"Say, what's this?" Bill exclaimed.

Fiona and Jack turned to see what he was talking about. He was standing near the edge of the rushing water and held up a length of braided rawhide.

"This is a piece of halter for a burro." He stepped to the side. "Here's some more..." The bank abruptly crumbled beneath his foot, casting him into the swiftly flowing stream. He dropped his torch, hissing into the water.

Bill reached for the edge, his fingers clawed at the loose dirt on top of the rock shelf, as the water pulled at him with irresistible force.

"Bill!" Fiona screamed as she dived to the ground, reaching out to grab his hand.

Their fingertips touched for a brief agonizing moment in time, as the current pulled him away from the edge and out into the channel. In a matter of seconds, he disappeared under the wall.

"Bill, Bill," she screamed again.

Fiona slowly got to her feet as she and Jack stared at each other for a long moment in sheer shock.

"Oh, my God in Heaven," whispered Jack.

"Where does this come out?" Fiona asked as she pointed at the rushing water.

"'Bout a quarter mile down the mountain. We rode past it jest before we got to Mary's cave."

Fiona stared at the rushing water where it disappeared under the wall for a moment and furrowed her forehead. "Give me your ropes."

Jack raised his eyebrows. "What fer?"

"I'm going after him."

"Are you crazy?"

"I've been accused of it, yes...Now take those ropes off," she said as she pulled hers over her head.

He handed her the two lariats. She took the dally end of her riata, stuck it through the loop of one of the others and tied a bowline knot. Fiona repeated the process until she had all three tied together—a little over a hundred and five feet.

She unbuckled her gunbelt, laid it on the cave floor, and then slipped the noose over her head and pulled it down to her waist. "See that column over there next to the outflow?...Get behind it and feed the rope out. If the creek doesn't emerge into another cave by the time I get to the end...I'll jerk twice and you can pull me back...hopefully."

"An' if'n I cain't?"

"Now that's a silly question...But I have no doubt you'll be able to. That's why I suggested you get behind that rock column...you can winch me or preferably both of us out."

Jack shook his head. "This is about the most foolhardy thing I ever heard. You got a hole in yer screen door you could drive a wagon through, lady...No offense."

"Like I said, been accused of that before...and none taken." She looked at him in the flickering torch light. "Bill's my friend, Jack. I can't just stay here and do nothing...Gotta at least try."

He nodded. "Yeah, mind I'd do the same if'n it was Bass or vice-e-versa...Shore wish he was hear."

"Me too...All right, it's time...Let's do it."

She sat on the rock ledge that formed the bank of the creek, snugged the rope tight around her waist and picked up one of the unused torches she had also laid on the floor.

"You gonna carry that? What good's that gonna do?...It'll be wet."

She nodded. "I know, but it's soaked in coal oil and pitch and I've got my flint and steel in my parfleche pouch. If I'm lucky and find Bill maybe I can get it to light and look for another way out."

"Yer askin' fer an awful lot of luck in one chunk."

Fiona grinned. "Shakespeare once said, 'Fortune brings in some boats that are not steered'."

"Awright, let's see if'n we kin steer this'un."

"Keep tension on the rope, if I find the tube opens, or an air pocket, I'll tug once. That'll mean hold what you have, so either I can take a breath or figure out if I'm in another cave."

175

"Can do."

She slipped into the water, drew a sharp intake of air and pushed herself into the current.

"Oh, my goodness, this is cold."

"Coulda told you that," he said as he played out a coil at a time.

Fiona's head disappeared under the rock wall…

HONEY MOUNTAIN

Bodie brought Winchester's black physician's valise back into the campsite and set it down beside him. "What else do you need me to do?"

"I'm gonna need a walking stick. You can go cut me a dogwood sapling while I clean this."

Bodie headed over to the clump of dogwood trees, unsheathing his Bowie on the way.

Winchester glanced at him walk away, and then reached down and pulled his bloody sock off. He studied the wound for a moment, took two gauze pads and covered the entry and exit holes. He held pressure for a few moments until much of the bleeding had stopped.

"Good thing I'm still flexible," he mumbled as he inspected the entry for contaminants and pieces of leather from his boot. "Looks clean."

He reached back in his bag for a small bottle of alcohol, removed the cap and started to pour some of the clear liquid in the wound. "No, better have Bodie do this…Angle's not right."

He looked up as the young ranger walked back with a five foot length of dogwood. Bodie was still shaving the small branches from the shaft.

"That can wait a moment, son. Need you to pour this alcohol directly into the hole. Hopefully some of it will go all the way through." He handed him the bottle and propped his foot on a melon-sized rock.

"You sure?" Bodie asked. "Gonna burn like all git out."

"Better that than get an infection and loose my entire foot."

"Good point." He handed the Chickasaw one of the limbs he cut from the staff. "You might want to bite on this."

"I think so. Take too long for Laudanum to take effect." He took the finger-sized stick and clamped down on it with his teeth and nodded.

Bodie turned the green bottle up and dribbled the liquid directly into the bullet hole. Winchester arched his back and groaned as both ends of the stick fell from his mouth.

Son cocked his head and whined.

"More," *Anompoli Lawa* croaked after he spat the remains of the stick out. "Until you see it come out of the bottom.

He poured some more and watched the sole of Winchester's foot. "There it is…Came through."

The elderly physician blew through his teeth several times until he could talk again. "All right, take some of that white salve from that small jar and put it in both wounds."

"Angie's turpentine and tallow, right?"

He nodded and wiped the sweat from his brow with his sleeve. "Uh, huh...Worked pretty well on the hole in your chest."

"It did that," he said as he packed both wounds with the salve.

"Now take two more of those pads from my bag and that roll of cotton cloth and bandage it. We'll have to wait till we get back to the house to fix a splint...Broke the second metacarpal. Thank God it wasn't the first."

"Why's that?" Bodie asked as he got the materials and did as he was instructed.

"The big toe is at the end of the first metacarpal. You get most of your balance from it...There is a small pouch of pins in there to anchor the wrapping."

He held up two safety pins. "Way ahead of you, Uncle." He secured the end of the bandage where it wrapped around Winchester's ankle.

"Good job...Well, we know one thing."

"What's that?"

"We're at the right place."

"How's that?"

"The Spirit Guardians were here. They were protecting the site...It's a good thing they knew me."

"Guess we'll know what's down there when Jack and them get back," said Bodie as he looked over at the entrance.

MCGANN HOME

Ruth Ann and Baby Sarah ran up to the gate in the white picket fence in a screaming panic, opened it and ran into the yard. Jim laid his book on the porch and got to his feet as he saw blood spattered on both of them.

"What's wrong? What happened? Are you all right?"

"Daddy, Daddy!...We're all right." Ruth Ann threw her arms around the tall man's legs.

The front screen door opened and Angie rushed out drying her hands on a dish towel. "Faith an' what's goin' on here? Whose blood is that?"

"We were almost attacked, Daddy. A big man tried to take Baby Sarah and..."

"Whoa, whoa, slow down, honey. Who tried to take Baby Sarah?...What do you mean, 'almost'?...Slowly now."

Ruth Ann took a deep breath and exhaled. "Three really ugly men, one huge, one kinda thick and the other was little with squinty eyes. They tried to take Baby Sarah...said they wanted Mister McGann and would hold her until he got back."

"Why did they want me husband?"

Ruthie looked at Angie. "I don't know, Miz McGann, because Boy attacked the big man when he went to hit me and killed him, and then killed the little one with the weasel eyes."

"Boy? Son's daddy?" exclaimed her father. "The one we saw in the woods on the way here?"

She nodded. "He jumped out from behind us and killed the two of them and the fat looking one ran off frightened and screaming his head off."

"That's when ya'll ran back here to the house?"

Ruth Ann shook her head. "No…A girl about my age came from around a big tree and put her arm over Boy's shoulders and told him it was all right now. She said they were there to protect us…Doctor Ashalatubbi said that Boy was a Spirit Guardian."

"Who was the little girl and where is she?" asked her puzzled father as he looked back down the path.

"She said her name was Anna."

Baby Sarah waved her hands around, bobbed her head and smiled big. "Ann-uh."

Angie gasped, sat down hard in one of the other chairs and covered her mouth with one hand.

§§§

CHAPTER NINE

THE CAVE

Fiona took a deep breath just before she had to duck under the rock wall. She held her hand up and let her fingers brush along the ceiling of the tube feeling for an air pocket—nothing.

Jack slowly played out the rope as a feeling of dread overtook him. *Why did I let her do this?* he thought. *Not that I could stop her, though.* The force of the water pulling on her body was immense and he braced himself against the travertine column for support. He looked down at the remaining coils of rope. *Dang, only another eight feet er so left.*

Fiona was running out of air in the ice cold water, her lungs strained to breathe, as she fought against the rising impulse to panic. *Oh, God, please, please let there be an opening*, she prayed. The blackness closed in as she started seeing stars. Her lungs neared bursting and unconsciousness was only seconds away...

Air! Her fingers couldn't feel the ceiling above her and there was a difference in the temperature surrounding her hand. She arched her back, tugged once to let Jack know to stop playing out the rope, as she exhaled and stuck her face above the surface of the water. Fiona took several deep draughts of the sweet air and reached as high as she could over her head and felt emptiness.

Her feet could touch the gravely bottom. She gave the rope another single tug to let Jack know to let her lifeline play out some more against the stiff current, as she pushed her way to the right, reaching out with her hand in the stygian darkness of the cave for the side wall.

Thank you, Jesus, she musta found some air, but is it another cave er just a pocket at the top? He eased out another coil—two left...

Her fingers touched a ledge and she pulled herself to it, clambered up on top and laid there a moment, panting, while she caught her breath.

"It's about time," a voice from the blackness startled her and she sat up.

"Bill! Where are you?"

"Right next to you. You brushed against my foot when you were crawling up on this shelf."

She reached over and felt his boot, and then his leg. He was sitting with his knees drawn up tightly against his chest and his arms wrapped around them.

"Oh, thank God," she said, as they embraced in the dark.

"Did you fall in, too?"

"No, I tied three ropes together and Jack's holding on to the other end."

"Now, that's not the brightest thing you've ever done."

"Jack said something real close to that."

"You don't actually think he can pull the both of us back through that tunnel against the current, do you?"

"Well, I did until I got in it…Have you been able to tell anything about this cave?"

"Not much. Felt around and this shelf we're on keeps going, don't know how far…But it's darker than the inside of a cow…"

She interrupted. "Just a minute…Here, hold this."

"What is...Hey, this is one of the torches. Now, what good's this gonna do? It's wet."

"You and Jack must have gone to the same school...he said that, too...Just hold it."

She dug in her parfleche pouch and pulled out a piece of flint the size of a spearhead and a small flat steel bar almost as big as a pocket knife.

Doing every thing by feel, Fiona positioned Bill's hands so the torch head was between her knees. She held the flint against it with her left hand and struck it sharply with the edge of the steel bar in her right—sparks flew. They sizzled out on the damp burlap. She struck it again, with the same effect.

"See? No way you're going to light it."

"Oh, ye of little faith."

Fiona felt the torch head until she found an area where the pine pitch was thicker. She put the piece of flint directly against the resin and struck again. A spark stuck to the sticky sap, but died. She repeated the procedure. This time, the spark stayed alive and began to smolder. Fiona cupped her hands around the glowing ember as it slowly grew.

The pine sap sizzled and started to burn, giving off an odor of turpentine along with a tendril of dark smoke. The flame crawled across the wrapped burlap like sorghum leaking from a barrel on a cold day, slowly burning the moisture away.

In a little over two minutes, the entire torch head was aflame, casting flickering shadows on the cavern walls and giving off a modicum of warmth to the shivering pair.

Bill shook his head and grinned. "Well, I'll be...From now on, if you say a hen dips snuff, I'm going to start looking under her wing for the can."

"Don't know about that, Marshal, but, I do know that pine resin will burn most any time you have something to start it with." She got to her feet and slipped the rope from her waist and over her head. "Now, let's see where this cave leads."

Jack felt the rope go slack and pulled slightly on it...it didn't tighten. *What in hell?* He tugged again and it went completely limp. *Jesus, Mary and Joseph...she's gone.* He coiled the three ropes back in and just stared at the empty loop on the end.

CADDO CREEK

John Olinger poured himself a cup of coffee from the tin pot and set it back next to the fire. He looked at Wheeler. "You say a big white wolf kilt Rizzo and Posey?"

"Quicker'n you kin say scat."

"An' you just ran?"

"Jest as fast as I could. That big-assed wolf wuz not only mean, but they wuz somethin' spooky 'bout him…It's like he come outta nowheres."

"Sounds like them same wolves up on the mountain what kilt Dudley," said Mo Brown.

"I even shot one an' he jest growled at me."

"Meby you ain't as good a shot as you think, Chaney."

The gunhawk glared at Olinger. "Any time you want to try me…"

"Later…The bossman ain't gonna be happy that we're comin' up empty-handed."

The doc, marshal an' them others gotta know somethin' or they wouldn't be a lookin' around in the same place we are," said Wheeler.

"What I don't git is all them white wolves. Ain't never seen 'ny wolves that big…not to say nothin' of bein' white with weird gold eyes," commented Chaney.

"Yeah, well, they're just wolves…Get it?…Wolves. We start carryin' our long guns when we go back up there…To my way of thinkin' they're trained to guard the treasure."

"Then how's come that one kilt Rizzo an' Posey? They's only them little girls around," said Wheeler.

"How do you know he didn't kill them kids after you run off like a scalded dog?" asked Olinger.

Wheeler glanced around at the others. "Well, I don't…But, if'n they's trained to guard the treasure…who the hell trained 'em?"

THE CAVE

Fiona led the way, holding the torch high over her head. Sometimes they had to crawl on their bellies and other times, turn sideways when the cave pinched down. The creek had disappeared again under the wall.

"How far do you think we've gone," asked Bill.

"Hard to tell the way the cave meanders about…I'll guess at least over a quarter of a mile.

"Yeah, that might be only a hundred yards or so topside."

The ceiling of one cavern they came to ten minutes later was over fifteen feet above their head and festooned with thousands of white straws sticking down like thick upside down hairs.

"Oh, look at that, another speleothem," said Fiona

"A what?"

"Speleothem…A cave structure formed by minerals and water like those three elephants, the blanket and curtains we saw earlier…Looks like a throne…How interesting."

They walked closer to the unique four-by-eight, by-six-foot structure.

"Hold the torch closer," said Bill.

She held the flame close to the glasslike surface. "Oh, my Lord," whispered Fiona. "That's the most amazing thing I've ever seen."

They walked around the chair-like formation, holding the torch close all the way. As if on cue, they both looked up at the myriad straws overhead—each was dripping one single drop of water every few seconds down on the throne and a wide area around it

"It's the gold," Fiona said softly.

"The bars are entirely covered with a thin, almost transparent, layer of travertine," Bill said, with awe in his voice.

"Can't be more than a quarter of an inch thick," she commented.

"Look at the way they stacked the ingots in two terraces, it gives it the appearance of a big wide chair...or throne," he added.

"And the nearly four hundred years of the mineralized water dripping down coated it like a layer of wax." Fiona ran her hand over the slick wet surface.

"Another one or two hundred more years and the travertine would be too thick to see through."

"Think they stacked them like this on purpose?" asked Fiona.

Bill shook his head. "No way of knowing…Another one of those coincidences?"

They looked at one another.

Fiona jerked her head up toward the darkened end of the tunnel. "What's that?"

Bill looked in the same direction to see a pale blue glow disappear around a bend in the cave. "What the…"

HONEY MOUNTAIN

Jack worked his way back up the rubble ramp to the campsite. He had Fiona's guns draped over his shoulder and carried the three lariats in his left hand.

Winchester sat with his back against a large boulder and his bandaged foot resting on a smaller rock.

"Uncle! What happened to your foot?" asked Jack, as he stepped out of the cave entrance.

Bodie came from back around the boulder with an armload of wood. "We had visitors."

Jack glanced over at his godson. "Visitors?"

"Couple of those miscreants that you sent to my office along with four others," said Winchester.

"Yeah, but, what happened to yer foot?" He pointed.

"The leader shot me because I wouldn't tell him who ya'll were."

Jack looked over at Bodie. "Where were you, sunshine?"

"I was out gatherin' up firewood down the mountain a ways when they rode up. Wadn't much I could do, but as it turned out Boy's kin kindly took care of things."

"Whoa, whoa...Yer gonna have to be a little more specific..."

Five minutes later, Bodie and Winchester had filled Jack in with the details.

"Now it's your turn. Where's Fiona and Bill?" asked Doctor Ashalatubbi.

Jack slipped the guns from his shoulder and laid the ropes beside them. "Well, grab yer butts, my story's worse than ya'lls..."

"Oh, Lord have mercy," Bodie exclaimed after Jack had told them what happened down below. "So now what?"

"Is there any chance they could come out somewhere else?" asked Winchester.

"Damn'f-I-know...What with probably over five miles of caves followin' that creek an' honeycombin' this mountain..."

"Sounds like Fiona had to purposely have taken the rope from her waist, don't you think?" commented *Anompoli Lawa*.

"That's my thinkin'…Tells me she found Bill and they knew I'd never pull 'em back through that small tunnel against the current…"

"So they took out lookin' fer another way. But they cain't see…Gotta be black as pitch," said Bodie.

"She took a torch, but got no idee how she'd git it lit," stated Jack.

"Fiona is a very resourceful woman, Jack…Very resourceful indeed," added Doctor Ashalatubbi.

MCGANN HOME

Jim pushed his way to his feet and stepped inside the cabin. In just a short moment, he came back out wearing his cavalry side arm, a Colt Single Action Army .45, buckled around his waist.

"And where would ye be goin'?" asked Angie.

"Better go back up the trail and see about the bodies."

"Ye can't be bringin' 'em here…What with ye wounded side."

"I know, but I feel obligated to check on them. Could be still alive."

"Don't think so, daddy. Boy was, uh, very efficient," said Ruthie. "It was awful."

"How far up the trail were ya'll?" he asked.

"Not sure, but we were right next to a really big cottonwood that was just off the path."

"That would be about a hundred meters or so. Would ye be likin' me to go with ye?"

Jim shook his head. "No...Think you'd better stay here with the girls...just in case there's still any of them around. Do you have a firearm?"

"I have me 10 gauge double-barreled Remington."

"10 gauge? That's pretty big for a woman."

Angie got a wry grin on her face. "Ye'll have to ask me husband if I can use it or not."

"All right. If you say so." He grabbed the hickory cane that was leaning against one of the front porch posts and made his way down the steps.

"Come girls, let me get ye cleaned up of the blood spatters." Angie took both of the children inside.

Jim scanned the woods on both sides of the path all the way from the house to the big cottonwood. The first thing he saw was a boot sticking out of the brush on the right side. It was attached to the rest of a huge man's body.

His throat was completely torn out exactly like the teenagers he saw down near the Red River. "No other wounds," he mumbled.

A few feet away on top of some brambles, lay the body of a much smaller man. His throat too, was gone. The bodies were twisted in their final death contortions and there was blood sprayed on the foliage all around.

"Damn...Hellova way to die."

Captain Bryan could feel the bile rising up toward his mouth. He turned, shook his head and made his way back to the house.

"What did ye see?" Angie asked as he opened the screen door and stepped inside.

"Just what Ruth Ann said. One giant of a man...ugly as my grandpa's toe nails...and another smaller man who wouldn't win any prizes either...both had their throats torn out."

"Saints preserve us." Angie crossed herself. "Was the same way Boy took care of a couple of malefactors two years ago, it was...Ruthie's right, Boy is definitely efficient."

She glanced around at the surrounding woods outside. "I'll not be worryin' that there's any others about...Not with him comin' back to pay us a visit."

THE CAVE

Fiona and Bill moved in the direction where they saw the blue glow. They followed the cave around a sharp corner and came to a divergence—the tunnel forked.

"Now which way?" he asked.

Fiona looked both directions. "Shakespeare said, 'Go wisely and slowly. Those who rush, stumble and fall'."

Bill nodded. "Yeah, I know, Romeo and Juliet...My mother always said, 'If you come to a fork in the road...take it." He grinned.

Fiona shook her head. "Well, let's try this way." She cautiously led off to the right-hand tunnel.

They had gone a little over ten yards, when Fiona held out her arm blocking Bill who was to her right and slightly behind her.

"What?" He looked at her.

She pointed at the cave floor less than one foot in front of her—it disappeared. "Drop-off."

He looked over. "Holy Mother of God. Can't even see the bottom...That was close."

"Too close."

They turned around and retraced their steps back to the other tunnel.

"Well, it's obvious that wasn't it," Fiona said as she led off down the other branch.

"Wonder what that blue light was we saw back yonder?"

"Well, what I think…Look! There it is again," she said.

The glow was stronger this time, but moved at a steady pace away from them.

"Let's try to catch up," said Bill.

"Don't forget that drop-off back there."

"Oh, yeah, right…Good thinking."

"It's not disappearing like before."

"But, we're not getting any closer."

"Maybe we are. It seems brighter and I can just make out…Oh, my goodness." Fiona brought her left hand to her mouth.

"What?"

"It's *Bánushah Kuukuh Náttih*."

"Come again?"

"The Blue Water Woman. I talked to her in my sweatlodge vision with *Anompoli Lawa*, remember?"

"Right. Wonder what she's doing here?"

The blue shrouded image ahead turned and the beautiful Caddo maiden looked directly at Fiona with her antique gold eyes and motioned with her hand to the left, and then she faded into nothingness.

"Come on, she just showed us the way out."

Bill looked at the sputtering torch in Fiona's hand. "Its a good thing. I'd say we have no more than four or five minutes before that thing's burned out."

"Agreed," she said, as they reached the area where the apparition had vanished. "Look." She pointed to a narrow crevice in the side wall of the cave. "I can see light."

Fiona dropped the burned-out torch, turned sideways and worked her way into the crack. Bill followed as they squeezed along, brushing against the sides of the crevice.

"Hope we don't get stuck," he said.

"It's a good thing we're both fairly thin. Still it helps to exhale and take shallow breaths."

The crack made a right-hand turn, and then sharply back to the left and got a little more narrow before beginning to widen.

"I can see daylight," Fiona said, as she looked up. "…and smell fresh air."

They came to the front of the crevice where it opened out on a cliff face. The opening was blocked by a thick copse of junipers. She and Bill pushed their way through the branches and out into the open.

"Oh, thank God. I never thought I was claustrophobic, but now I'm not sure," she said as she sat down on the ground.

"Me too." He turned and looked back at the cliff. "You'd never know that entrance was there because of the cedars blocking the front. No wonder it's never been found...Wonder which way the campsite is?"

Fiona pointed up the hill. "Gotta be that way." She got back to her feet.

HONEY MOUNTAIN

Bodie picked up Fiona's gunbelt to lay it on the boulder with the hats. He pulled one of the pistols out of the holster, felt its balance and checked the cylinder. "Yep, didn't think there'd be one under the hammer."

He opened the gate and dumped the five .38-40 rounds in his hand, closed it and spun the cylinder. Bodie thumbed the hammer back to full cock, pointed at a tree up the hill and squeezed the trigger. "Dang, that's smooth. I'll bet it's less than two pounds on that trigger pull and looky here, Uncle Jack...See the hammer?"

Jack put his coffee cup down, stepped over to Bodie and took the weapon from him. "Son of a gun, hammer's been heat treated and flared to the outside...Huh, that makes it a lot easier and quicker to cock on the draw with the side of your thumb."

He dragged the edge of his thumb across the shaped hammer, dropping it into the cocked position, released it and repeated the procedure. "Unbelievable...Just like silk."

"The hammer on the left-hand gun is bent the opposite way, see?...Right hand, left hand." Bodie held it up. "Nice balance too." He twirled it on his index finger, flipped it into his grip and thumbed the hammer back in one continuous motion.

"Well, Fiona's the third person I ever seen could use two guns equally well...Bass was the first," said Jack.

"Who was the second?"

"Johnny McCabe."

"You know Johnny McCabe?" Bodie asked in awe.

Jack nodded. "Me an' Bass worked with him back in '82, believe it was. He was a Texas Ranger, you know?"

"Oh, hell, yeah. Daddy told me they called him the Gunman of the Rio Grande...the original gunhawk." He chuckled. "Boy howdie, can you imagine, Bass Reeves, Johnny McCabe and Fiona Miller all in one place? That would scare ever outlaw in the territory half to death."

Jack laughed. "Yeah, be like Belle Starr runnin' in to give herself up to Bud Ledbetter when she heard it was Bass Reeves had paper on her."

"Johnny McCabe and Bass Reeves...Haw! Who'd a thunk?"

"What about Johnny McCabe and Bass Reeves?" said a voice from the other side of the boulder Winchester was leaning against.

Jack, Bodie and Winchester all turned as Bill and Fiona came around the big rock.

"Well, let's hallelujah the county...Gotta say, ya'll er a sight fer sore eyes." Jack shook Bill's hand and slapped him on the shoulder, and then hugged Fiona. "Thought the both of you wuz gonners fer shore."

"Good to see ya'll too," said Bill.

"And yes, we'll take some hot coffee." Fiona pointed at the pot next to the fire. "These doeskins are still damp from my swim in the creek...Like to have froze to death."

She walked over and held out her hands over the flames. "What happened to your foot, Doctor Ashalatubbi?"

"I'll explain later...How the deuce did ya'll get out?" he asked.

"Coffee first, then we'll tell you...May take a while." Bill looked at Fiona, and then back at the others. "Not sure you're going to believe it...Hell, not sure we do."

She glanced at Bodie and grinned. "Were you figuring on inheriting my pistols, Bodie?"

"Oh...Golly, no, Ma'am...I mean Fiona. Uh, Jack brought 'em back up with him and I was jest puttin' 'em over next to your hat...Just thought I'd check the trigger pull an' such." He thumbed the five shells back in her right-hand gun and slipped it into its holster. "Boy, those are nice…really nice…Smoother'n a greased baby's butt."

Fiona grinned again. "Thank you. I can show you how to customize yours, if you want."

"Wow, that would be great, Fiona. Really great…They could use some work awright."

"What was all this ya'll were talking about with Bass and McCabe?" asked Bill.

"Aw, I just mentioned Bass an' me worked with him back a few years ago."

"Interesting. Johnny and I also crossed paths a time or two…along with his brothers Joe and Matt," commented Bill.

"Care to tell us about it?" asked Bodie.

"Some other time. Got other things to talk about…like gold."

"Ya'll found it?" exclaimed Bodie.

Bill stuck out his cup and grinned. "Coffee."

§§§

CHAPTER TEN

MCGANN HOME

"You don't think those miscreants can find that passageway that leads to the throne room?" asked Bodie, as they walked from the paddock after unsaddling their mounts.

Fiona shook her head. "Not likely. It's been there for many, many years and no one has found it yet. Besides, only someone as svelte as Bill and I could get through...You and Jack wouldn't have a chance."

"Svelte? What in the world is svelte?"

She grinned. "Stylishly slim."

"Oh, you mean skinny."

She backhanded him against his shoulder.

Ken Farmer

They opened the yard gate and walked up to the wide covered front porch.

Angie ran down the steps to help Winchester. "Uncle, ye be hurt. What happened?" she asked, as she took his elbow and helped him up the steps.

He glanced at the sidearm buckled about Jim's waist. "I'd say we both have some tales to tell…Starting with those two bodies we passed on the trail from the falls."

Later, they were all sitting out on the porch with fresh cups of coffee. Fiona had changed from her still slightly damp doeskins into her regular wear and hung them out on Angie's clothesline. The children were playing with Baby Sarah's rag dolls on the deck.

Jack was sitting on the steps, while Doctor Ashalatubbi was in one of the rockers with his foot propped up on a three-legged milking stool.

"Well, that's purty much our story," said McGann. "'Peers as though Boy an' them other wolves saved all our bacon to a fair-thee-well."

"Not to say anything about the Blue Water Woman," said Fiona. She glanced over at *Anompoli Lawa*. "Do you think that Boy could be part of the therianthropy or the Spirit Guardians?"

"The what?" asked a confused Bodie.

"Shapeshifters…The wolves."

He shook his head and mumbled, "Don't know why folks cain't jest talk American."

"Spirit Guardians, yes, therianthropy of the Caddo…no. Boy is here through the Chickasaw and Anna to protect her mother, Jack and now Baby Sarah…The Caddo Guardians, through the Blue Water Woman, are here to protect the Atakapan Tejas Caddo heritage which includes the burial sites…and the treasure."

He blew across the surface of his coffee and took a sip. "Would loved to have seen *Bánushah Kuukuh Náttih*, again," added *Anompoli Lawa*.

Bodie shook his head. "That would be a sight to behold…"

"The Blue Water Woman?" asked Jack.

"Well, that too, but, seein' all that gold encased in rock…"

"That's where it's going to stay. The only way to get to it is through the water cave underground Bill and I went through or that tiny crack in the cliff," said Fiona.

"Should we close that access?" asked Bill.

"Could," said Jack. "It'd take somebody skinny enough to shade themselves under a clothesline to git through like Fiona said…but, they could always come back an' widen the crevice with minin' tools…'Course that ain't agonna happen long as I'm around."

"Then, again, if it did, I'm afraid they'd have to deal with the lycanthropes," said Winchester.

"The what?" asked Jack.

Doctor Ashalatubbi glanced at the marshal. "The shapeshifting Spirit Guardians...the Dire Wolves."

"Oh, like Boy...Why didn't you say so."

Winchester nodded. "I did...Only they're bigger...much bigger."

"Great jumpin' Jehoshaphat! Boy is purtnear a hunderd an' eighty pounds his ownself," commented Jack.

"True enough...His cousins are well over two hundred, probably closer to three." Doctor Ashalatubbi took another sip of his coffee. "Not to broach a distasteful subject, but we have three bodies we need to take care of...and soon."

Son got to his feet growling and looking off toward the road.

"May be havin' a bit of the help," said Angie as she glanced up and saw Deputy US Marshals Selden Lindsey and Loss Hart, along with new Chickasaw Lighthorse, Alex Sixkiller, ride in from the wagon road.

"Well, looky here, looky here what the cat drug in," said Jack getting up from the steps as the three lawmen reined to a halt. "What brings ya'll out thisaway? On the scout for some evildoers?"

Selden and Loss exchanged glances as they dismounted and tied their horses to the hitching rail outside the fence. Sixkiller stayed mounted.

"Fer those of you other than Doc Ashaltubbi, this here's Alex Sixkiller, he was Ben's brother...New Chicksaw Lighthorse...Jest as well git down, Alex," said Lindsey.

"*Sheeah, Yahash Losa Ombi Pisali*," said Winchester.

"*Sheeah, Anompoli Lawa*," the Chickasaw said as he too, dismounted.

"What does his Indian name mean?" asked Bill.

"Black Buffalo Sees Rain."

"Got a complaint on you, Jack," said Selden. The broad-shouldered, mustachioed marshal removed his wide-brimmed pinched-top black hat and nervously wiped his brow with his kerchief. "How do." He nodded at the others on the porch.

He opened the spring-loaded gate in the white picket fence and they entered the yard.

"'Bout what?"

Lindsey returned everybody's stare on the porch, looked at Jack and put his hat back on his head. "Uh, some fellers said yer dogs kilt three of their friends up here."

Jack looked at Selden for a long minute, glanced over at Loss, and then back. He chuckled. "You've got to be jestin'...Them worthless nabobs got more try than a Baptist preacher." He chuckled again. "They come up on our property…trespassin' mind you…shot Uncle Winchester in the foot, whilst me, Fiona and Brushy Bill was down in a cave up on the mountain."

He pointed at Doctor Ashalatubbi up on the porch with his bandaged foot propped up. "An' to top that, three more of 'em tried to kidnap Baby Sarah…Well, I'm here to say that Boy put an abrupt stop to that foolishness."

"Hmm, they didn't say nothin' 'bout that," said Selden as his cheeks blushed.

"Hell! That don't surprise me one bit…Reminded me when that shyster Baldwin from Ardmore, sent the Sartain brothers an' their gang up here two year ago…If'n they come back, we're gonna do the same thing we done then…If'n you'll recall, you, Loss an' Black Buffalo's brother Ben, wuz helpin' out in that little fandango."

Selden nodded. "I know, Jack, I know. They made the complaint and we had to come up here and check it out. You can understand that."

He pulled out a folded piece of paper from his suit coat pocket and held it up.

Jack took it from his fingers, pulled a Lucifer from his vest pocket, lit it with his thumbnail and set the paper on fire. When it got close to his fingers, he dropped it to the ground and snuffed out the flames with the heel of his boot.

"There...Takes care of that complaint."

Selden gave him a meek smile. "Figured it might be somethin' like that when I seen that one of 'em was that smarmy gunhawk, Hayden Chaney."

"Yeah, that snake has tried to brace me twict."

Angie got to her feet up on the porch. "Well, Selden, since it's near noon, ye, Loss, an' Alex just as well stay fer lunch. Got a big pot of squirrel stew on me stove...an' a dewberry cobbler in the oven."

"You mean it's lunch time already?" exclaimed Loss as he pulled out his pocket watch from his vest, popped open the cover and glanced at it.

"As if ye didn't know, Loss Hart...ye blatherskite. Ye can go wash up on the back porch before ye come into me house...After ye put the horses in the paddock an' give 'em some hay. The poor creatures don't need to be standin' out here tied to me railin'."

"Thankee ma'am," the three lawmen said at the same time.

The group sat around the long dining table as Angie dished out big dollops of dewberry cobbler in front of each person and added a dash of fresh sweet cream on top. The children ate at the breakfast table in the kitchen.

Loss bent over his bowl and sniffed the steaming desert. "Mmm, mmm. Dang if'n this don't smell purtnear too good to eat, Angie."

"Faith an' I can take it back if ye be wantin'."

He jerked upright. "No, no...Think I kin handle it...Fact is..."

"I know, ye just might be havin' seconds...This isn't the first time ye've eaten at me table, Loss Hart."

He grinned at the attractive redhead. "Yessum."

"What were those yahoos a doin' up here anyways?" Selden asked Jack as he dipped into his cobbler.

CADDO CREEK

"Did you file that complaint with the local marshal's office, Olinger?"

The barrel-chested man pitched the remains of his coffee into the fire with a hiss. "I done just like you said Boss...We watched from down the street when Lindsey and his partner rode out of town toward the Arbuckles."

"Not that it'll do much good, but it did buy us enough time for me to get up here." The nattily-dressed leader stepped down from his steel-dust American Standardbred stallion, removed his black kidskin gloves, and handed the reins to

Rube Monohan. "Take him down to the creek and let him drink…Not too much. He's worth more than you are."

He looked back at the four other men who had ridden up from Gainesville with him. "You boys get down and take care of your horses. They'll need to be rested for what we have to do later."

The four hired guns nodded, dismounted and followed Rube down to the creek.

Chaney handed the man with the silver temples a fresh cup of coffee.

He took the blue graniteware cup without any acknowledgment at all and sipped some of the stout trail brew. His face wrinkled. "Apparently you can't make coffee any better than you can do what you're told."

"Boss, we…"

He glared at Olinger. "I don't want to hear it…It has became painfully quite obvious you jackasses aren't capable of functioning on your own, so I came myself and brought some additional guns with me."

Olinger shuffled his feet. "So, what's the plan?"

He took another sip of his coffee, pitched the remainder on the ground, and then flipped the cup back to Chaney. "We take out the whole bunch, at one time."

"The women and kids too?"

Ken Farmer

The leader's thunderstorm blue eyes snapped at Wheeler. "Jesus Christ, man, that's what I'm talking about. I have to lead you bunch of morons around by the hand...Would you like me to get you a sugar tit, too?...I don't want any interference what so ever from anyone...Is that clear?"

He took a dark Cuban cigar from his inside coat pocket, unwrapped and clipped the end. "It's taken me years to research and set up this operation to find that missing Spanish gold." He lit up and took a big draw.

"What about them wolves?" asked Olinger.

The leader exhaled a big cloud of blue aromatic smoke over his head. "That's why I brought these additional four men...They're all experienced big game hunters in addition to being gunhands." He sneered, causing his Van Dyke to twist a little to the side. "They're all carrying Winchester or Marlin .45-70 long guns, loaded with hollowpoints...They'll bring down an African lion."

"How're we goin' in?" asked Wheeler.

"I checked the maps, there's only two entrances to that valley...Coming from the Davis side to the north and the Poolville side to the south...Wheeler, you take Brown, Allison and Monohan and go in from the north...Olinger, you and Chaney come with me and my other men. We'll come in the south way...and meet at the McGann house...Rube, bring my horse here."

210

"Yessir," the pockmark-faced smallish man replied as he led the stallion up to the boss.

He undid the saddlebags from behind the cantle and slung them over to Wheeler. "Here, you know how to use this?"

Monte unbuckled the straps on one side, looked in the pouch and staggered back a couple of steps. "Good Godalmighty...dynamite! What if'n I'd a dropped it?"

He shook his head. "It's like Mister Shakespeare said, Wheeler, 'The common curse of mankind, folly and ignorance, be thine in great revenue!'"

"Huh?"

"The time to worry is if you see the sticks begin to sweat."

MCGANN HOME

After Jack, Fiona and Doctor Ashalatubbi had filled everyone in on the details of the last week, Lindsey glanced over at Loss and the Lighthorse.

"What do ya'll think? Reckon we oughta hang around a bit?"

"I'd say so," said Loss. "Them nefarious nabobs is on a first-name basis with the bottom of the deck."

The Chickasaw Lighthorse, Alex Sixkiller nodded. "Uhnn, Sixkiller stay."

"So, how's it gonna be Jack, this here's yore territ'ry."

McGann nodded. "Well, been givin' it a right smart of thought since we got back."

"Uh, oh," said Bodie.

He snapped a sharp glance at his godson. "Watch it, slick."

Bodie grinned. "Well, Uncle Jack, you know what Bass always said 'bout you thinkin'."

"Well, Bass ain't here today...They's no question in my mind but what them owlhoots is comin' back. They somehow know 'bout that gold up in the cave...They jest don't know 'xactly where it is....The real question is when an' how they's comin' in."

"We're not all going to be here at the house are we?" asked Bill.

"Not hardly. That wouldn't be militarily smart...Would it Captain?"

"Not in my opinion," he replied. "Sun Tzu said in the Art of War, 'Attack him where he is unprepared, appear where you are not expected'."

"Who?" asked Bodie.

"Sun Tzu, a great Chinese general we studied at West Point."

"Right."

Jack continued, "We scattered out when the Sartain gang come an' we're gonna do the same today." He looked at

Bodie. "Sunshine, since you ain't one hundered percent, I want you up in the loft over the barn with yer long gun...You kin see most everthing 'tween the road an' the house from there in case they try to git close enough to use dynamite."

"Gotcha, Uncle Jack." Bodie got his extra ammo from his saddlebags, grabbed his Winchester and headed to the door.

"Need 'ny help climbin' the ladder?" asked Jack.

Bodie frowned at the sarcasm. "Think I can handle it."

McGann watched him exit the back door. "Now, let's see...Selden, you take Loss and Black Buffalo and cover the north entrance to the valley...Scatter out where you think ya'll do the most good...You may run across the mounts belongin' to them two bodies up the path. "

"Do you want to move their sorry carcasses to the barn?" asked Loss.

"Oh, hell no. Stink it up? No thankee...Leave 'em lay fer now, be a good warnin' fer the rest."

"Easy enough," said Lindsey as he motioned to Loss and the Lighthorse.

"Jim, you an' Uncle Winchester, bein' the walkin' wounded, will pertect the house with Angie and the girls...Hon, first shot you hear, you git the babies into the cave at the back of the house...I'll leave Son here. He'll let you know if somebody's a gittin close."

"You have a cave at the back?" asked Jim.

213

Angie nodded. "There was a mine into the cliff when me an' me first husband, God rest his soul, first came to the valley. We built this house against the cliff so we could use the cave if need be...There were more than a few renegades roamin' the country back then...There's a two-inch thick oak door built into the entrance...It's in me pantry off the kitchen and behind a curtain...We use it mostly for a fruit celler." She pointed to the back.

"Well, I'll be jiggered," said Bill as he laced up his tall Apache moccasins.

"Huh, see you been schooled by Bass, too," said Jack.

"Actually it was Fiona...she was schooled by Bass."

Jack grinned. "Wern't we all...Oh, Jim, you got yer cavalry side arm an' you kin use my Marlin .45-70, if'n you need it...Angie's got her ten gauge and Uncle Winchester, they's a brand new pump-action twelve gauge over 'side the front door...It holds five rounds."

The Chickasaw Shaman nodded. "I can handle that. I'll set my chair near the front window...Angie, would you mind going ahead and putting my carpet bag in your fruit cellar? It has those artifacts we mentioned."

"Of course, Uncle." She picked up the bag and headed back toward the kitchen.

"Ya'll be sure to swing the windows in and close them thick wood shutters...They got shootin' slots in 'em. Don't think even a .45-70 round kin go through these cedar log walls."

Fiona walked back in from the spare bedroom in her doeskins, buckling her crossdraw gunbelt around her shapely hips. "You were right, *Anompoli Lawa*, they dried just fine...not stiff at all."

"I could tell they had been brain-tanned by your Cherokee grandmother. You can get them wet many times and they'll always dry butter soft."

"Fiona, why don't you come with me up to the top of the falls case any of 'em come over by way of Poolville...Bill, yer still jest a mite gimpy, you kin take the path 'tween here an' the falls."

"I'm all right, Jack, unless you want to run a foot race with me or somethin'."

He grinned. "Not today...but I'll keep it in mind."

McGann looked at the others still inside. "Awright, let's get on about it. Everbody be shore you got plenty ammo...Got enough to start a small war over in the sideboard...Take what you want."

"I'll leave my Winchester here, in case it's needed. Believe all my work will probably be of the close proximity kind," said Fiona as she thumbed a sixth round into each of her Peacemakers. She looked over at Jack and then at the door. "Shall we?"

"Give me a half a shake to git my moccasins an' lace 'em up."

HONEY MOUNTAIN

Wheeler, and the others reined up just off the rutted wagon road that led to the small community of Davis to the north.

"Let's leave the horses in that grove of 'simmon trees down yonder near the creek," said Wheeler. "Cain't go by road and the brush 'tween here an' the house is too thick fer horses...Big Jim you kin git up on that ridge on the west above the house from here."

He dug into the saddlebags and pulled out two sticks of dynamite. "When you git up top there, you oughta be jest about over the cabin. Be fair easy to drop these over the edge to the roof."

"How'm I gonna know when to drop 'em?"

Wheeler, Brown and Monohan exchanged glances.

"Uh...Well, when you git to the top an' are above that log house, then you go ahead an' light them sticks an' chunk 'em over the cliff...Kaboom! That oughta take care of them apples," said Wheeler. "Then we'll go in an' see if'n they's 'ny survivors...You got 'ny matches?"

Allison frowned at the smaller man. "Why shore. You think my momma raised a fool?"

"You don't want me to answer that." Wheeler motioned to the others to start working their way through the brush toward the house.

"Mo, you git over yonder on the other side of the ranch road next to the creek, an' me'n Rube'll take this here side…an' here, you and me will split the rest of the dynamite."

He handed Monohan two of the sticks.

"How far is it to the house?" asked Mo.

"I mind it's 'bout a quarter mile er better," answered Wheeler.

"We coulda rid our horses a mite closter."

"Why shore, coulda brung in a brass band too."

"I wuz jest thinkin'."

"I'll do the thinkin'…Now git movin'." He watched Brown cross the road and work his way through the green briars and whoa vines toward the creek. "Don't know sic 'em from come'ere," he mumbled, and then looked at Rube. "You spread out over there to the bottom of the cliff. I'll stay alongside the road. If'n you see one of them white wolves…shoot it."

The big steel-dust stallion picked his way through the finger-like gray granite outcrops sticking up through the thin

217

grass down the mountain toward the falls leading the others. They had crossed the seasonally low Honey Creek back a little more than thirty yards upslope.

The dapper rider in tan jodhpurs with canvas leggings and spats eased back on the reins. "This is far enough. We'll tie up here in that grove of sweet gum trees…Go the rest of the way on foot."

He looked over at his long gun shooters. "You boys work your way to higher ground. Chaney, Olinger and I will go down by the falls and up to the house from that direction."

They simultaneously looked up when they heard the shrill hunting cry of a bald eagle gliding on the thermals above their head. The six men failed to see the four sets of golden eyes scattered in a loose circle amongst the boulders about them, watching.

A beautiful Indian maiden in a pale-blue beaded doeskin dress also watched from the shadows of a limestone outcrop. Her long lustrous raven hair hung loosely in soft waves about her face with a single white underfeather from a bald eagle woven into it dangling next to her right ear. She glanced up at the soaring eagle—her golden eyes glimmered in the reflected light…

§§§

CHAPTER ELEVEN

HONEY MOUNTAIN

Lighthorse Alex Sixkiller sat unmoving—as only Indians can do—in his hide among some boulders on top of the cliff, directly above the McGann cabin. The top of the limestone ridge was well over a hundred and fifty feet above the floor of the valley. His keen hearing told him a large white man was noisily making his way up the steep slope to the top.

"White man make noise for many," Sixkiller mumbled.

Big Jim was puffing loudly as he neared the top of the ridge. He had climbed at an oblique angle to the west toward the house, instead of the much harder, but shorter route straight up.

When he reached the top, he bent over with his hands on his knees and tried to catch his breath. After several minutes, he straightened up, looked around and saw nothing but loose rocks and boulders. To the west, on some flat ground, was a small field with corn and field peas the McGanns had planted—the corn was in the tassel stage.

He moved down a narrow trail bordered by oak, pecan and sycamore trees along the ridgeline that led to the west, pausing every ten or fifteen yards, to look over the edge. He finally reached the area he figured should be above the house.

He peered over and could see the galvanized standing-seam roof down below through the mixed oak, hickory and cedar trees that grew on the slope.

Allison reached into his coat pocket, retrieved the two sticks of dynamite and twisted the five-inch fuzes together.

The Lighthorse moved silently through the scattered rocks toward the big man, knife in his hand. He watched as the white man pulled a match from his pocket, strike it across the seat of his canvas pants and held the twisted fuze above the flaring phosphorus Lucifer.

Sixkiller threw all caution away as he dropped his knife, palmed his Colt and aimed at the outlaw just as the big man drew back his arm to throw the lit sticks of dynamite…

Mo Brown cautiously eased his way down a game trail that ran alongside Honey Creek. His Smith and Wesson Russian revolver was gripped tightly in his hand.

"You must be lost, pilgrim," said Loss Hart, just loud enough to be heard over the gurgling of the stream as he stepped out from behind a large cottonwood. His Colt was aimed at Brown's chest.

"Son of a bitch!" Mo exclaimed as he thumbed the hammer back on his pistol.

That was his last act on this earth as Loss' Peacemaker roared and a .45 caliber slug slammed into the middle of his chest.

Brown's gun discharged into the dirt of the trail in front of him. He got a surprised expression on his face as he looked down at the dime-sized hole in his once white boiled shirt and the blood that was slowly spreading outward and down from the wound, saturating the material.

He looked up at Loss. "Aw, damn. Who are…" Then his eyes rolled back into his head and he tumbled sideways into the clear shallow water of the Honey.

"Deputy United States Marshal Loss Hart…an' you shouldn't oughta pointed yer gun at me." He watched Brown's body float downstream, staining the water around it a pale red, until it hung up on some willow roots.

Wheeler jerked at the sound of the two quickly spaced gunshots. "What in hell?"

"I'd say one of yore pals done got his self shot," said Marshal Lindsey as he stepped up behind the smaller man. "Now, git 'em up." He cocked his Colt for emphasis.

Both men were startled when the loud boom of an explosion echoed up and down the valley.

Alex Sixkiller had fired just as Allison's arm came forward, his bullet striking him in the side just below his armpit. The big man grunted and dropped to his knees as the two joined sticks of dynamite flipped end over end up into the air.

The deadly explosives struck a large limb hanging out over the trail and bounced back down, landing beside the kneeling wounded outlaw.

Big Jim's eyes got as big as saucers as he scrambled in a panic to pick up the sticks. He watched the sputtering, twisted fuze disappear into the tops of the cardboard cylinders just as his fingers closed around them—it would be the last thing he would ever see on this plane of existence.

The Lighthorse dove behind a chifforobe-sized granite outcrop, covering his ears as the dynamite exploded in a huge ball of fire and with a tremendous clap of thunder. Bits of rock, dirt, leaves, branches, smoke, blood and body parts were flung high into the air above the tree tops, and then rained down all about. Sixkiller jumped as a large smoking brogan shoe landed next to him—the big man's foot was still inside.

"Come along, girls," Angie said as she hustled the children into the cave. She had already lit several coal oil lanterns and placed a couple of Baby Sarah's dolls inside.

"Are the bad men coming, Miz McGann?" asked Ruth Ann.

"Yes, dear, but you and Baby Sarah will be safe in here," she said as she closed and latched the thick heavy door.

Angie rushed over, grabbed her ten gauge and was checking the loads when the exploding dynamite above rattled the dishes in her cupboard. "Faith and begorrah!…The rapscallions."

Jim levered a round into Jack's Marlin as Doctor Ashalatubbi racked the twelve gauge when debris started falling on the metal roof like a hail storm. They looked up at the vaulted ceiling, and then at each other.

"I'd say they're serious," said Jim. "That was dynamite."

Angie looked up again. "It came from the top of the ridge over me house, I'm thinkin'."

"The gunfire was from up north toward the Davis road," said Winchester.

Ken Farmer

"That would make it Marshals Lindsey and Loss and the Lighthorse," said Jim, with no little concern in his voice.

Angie stuck her head out the back door. "Are ye all right, Bodie Hickman?"

"Yessum. There was a hellova explosion up on top of the ridge…but I reckon you know that."

Jack, Fiona and Bill looked back to the north at the cloud of debris boiling up above the trees on top of the ridge.

"I'd say that was dynamite an' I'd say bein' up there on top of the ridge, that it was accidental er premature."

Fiona looked at McGann and nodded. "I'd have to agree with you, Marshal."

They heard a shrill cry overhead and looked up to see the big bald eagle bank and soar back toward the crest of the mountain.

The leader jerked his head up at the sound of the dynamite exploding. "There we go. That's what I've been waiting…" He saw the dark debris cloud on the top of the ridge. "Dammit to hell! Idiots, blithering idiots." He shook his head.

"There's nothin' up there, boss," said Olinger.

He glared at the barrel-chested man. "Fool. Don't you think I know that?"

Rube Monohan slipped by Selden while he was disarming Wheeler and shackling his hands around a tree trunk. He forced his way through the green briars and whoa vines until he was back down near the ranch road. "The hell with this."

He stepped out of the woods into the narrow road, keeping close to the edge and crept toward the house. Rube stopped at the corner of the red barn and studied the big log house for a moment. *If'n I run towards the corner 'nybody at the front winders cain't see me*, he thought.

Son got to his feet looking in the direction of the road outside. A deep rumbling growl emitted from his throat as the hair along his back rose.

"Visitors, people," said Jim, as he leaned up against the wall next to the shuttered window and peered out the shooting slot.

Angie scrunched down under the side window in the dining area and waited.

Rube took a deep breath, lit the dynamite and sprinted toward the house. He had covered almost half of the thirty-five yards when Angie rose up from the dining room window. At the same time, Bodie drew a bead on the man's back as he ran past the barn.

She quickly brought the big ten gauge to her shoulder, poked it through the slot and pulled both triggers. The recoil staggered her back a fortuitous several feet and to her butt.

Part of the load of twenty-four double ought buckshot hit the running man in the face, the rest hit the dynamite he was holding above his head preparatory to flinging it at the roof. Simultaneously, the ranger's shot from the loft hit him between the shoulders.

The tremendous explosion with its accompanying mushroom of fire and shock wave blew the shutters off the side windows of the house and could have seriously maimed or killed Angie if she hadn't already been knocked backward and to the floor.

"Boss, that come from the direction of the marshal's house," said Chaney.

He came to an abrupt halt in the game trail that ran down the mountain on the north side of the falls.

The boss and Olinger, immediately behind him, also stopped. A slow grin spread across the leader's face.

"Finally…One of those half-wits made it," he commented.

The sound of a big bore rifle sounded from back up the hill a little over two hundred yards.

He chuckled. "Well, things are looking up. One of my shooters must have taken out a wolf."

Another .45-70 shot echoed from a short distance to the north of the first.

"Ha! There's another one…See? What did I tell you boys?"

The first two shots were followed by the rapid fire of seven more—then silence.

"What in hell?" he said, looking around.

Atop several boulders above and to the north of the three men, two giant white wolves appeared, staring at the trio.

"Olinger! Shoot, damn you."

"Don't think I'd do that," came Jack's voice as he stepped from behind a large granite outcrop ten yards downhill.

Fiona and Bill followed immediately from their places of concealment near McGann.

Jack glanced at Chaney. "Well, gunhawk, we meet again."

Hayden got a wry grin on his face. "So we do, Marshal…'ceptin' this time ain't nobody around to pull me off." The young gunfighter's hand drifted down toward his swivel holster.

"I wouldn't say that," said Fiona softly.

He looked at the attractive brunette and chuckled. "Got a split-tail coverin' yer backside now?"

"I got this, Fio…"

She held up her left hand. "Uh, uh, Jack. Hate it when some misguided, hog-swilling excuse for a man calls me that."

227

Chaney snarled and hissed, "You worthless whore...I'll cut you in two." He swiveled his Colt at Fiona and pulled the trigger, but his shot buried in the ground, taking his big toe with it.

Two slugs, not an inch apart, had impacted his chest almost simultaneously a split second before his finger squeezed the trigger.

"I hate that word too," Fiona said, as she stood there with the gunsmoke cloud in front of her two Colts slowly dissipating in the afternoon breeze.

He looked down at the two holes, staining his ivory shirt and gray vest with his life's fluid. "Impossi..."

Chaney never finished his spoken thought as his knees buckled and he fell over backward, landing with a muted thud in the short curly buffalo grass.

"Olinger," the leader shouted.

Bill's eyes snapped to the stocky mustachioed man in the green bowler. "What'd he call you?"

"Olinger, why?...A dead man don't need to know names."

"You wouldn't be related to Bob Olinger back in New Mexico?"

"My uncle...Again, why?"

Bill's jaw muscles worked. "Apparently the apple doesn't fall very far from the tree. Had to kill that worthless, evil, dry-gulching bastard."

John squinted at Bill. "Who the hell are you?"

"Doesn't matter. I'm the man that's going to send you to perdition to join your uncle."

"What the hell are you talkin' 'bout?"

"Robert Olinger was a cold-blooded killer. His own mother, your great aunt, said he was a murderer from the cradle, and if there is a hell hereafter, then he is there…The bastard killed my friends by shooting them in the back. Said he was going to give me all twenty-four buckshot between my shoulder blades…I beat him to it and gave it to him in his face with his own shotgun…He died too quick."

Olinger's eyes got bigger. "Uncle Bob was murdered by Billy the Kid in '81…The Kid's dead. Pat Garr…Oh, God! It cain't be."

He reached for the Remington on his right hip. He never cleared leather.

Bill drew his Colt Frontier in a blur, triggering off the first round, and then fanning two more. All three .44-40 slugs hit the stocky man in the center of his chest—the holes could be covered by a playing card.

"And now there's only one," said Fiona as she looked at the leader, and then glanced up to see four giant, snarling white wolves gathering around them—each showed blood stains around their muzzles.

"Just who the hell are you?" asked Jack.

The man nervously removed his dark gray Homburg and wiped his sweating forehead with a white linen handkerchief from his vest pocket.

"Cuthbert Baldwin…"

"Gainesville's mayor?" Fiona said in surprise.

His chin went up. "I am…and you must be that female deputy."

She grinned. "You noticed…Now, one question…Why?"

He put his hand inside his hat to wipe the band. "There are two answers."

"Well, don't keep us waitin' all day, buttercup," said Jack.

"One, I'm a bit of an historian and I was doing some research. I discovered the story about the lost Spanish conquistador gold train stolen by the Atakapan Tejas Caddo…My findings led to this area."

He put his kerchief back in his pocket. "Answer two…and this one's personal." Baldwin looked at Jack and sneered. "This man and his Irish woman are directly responsible for Judge Parker hanging my older brother."

"Jason Baldwin was yer brother?…Hell, the shyster son of a bitch brought it down on his ownself. He kilt a bunch of gold miners, my partner…Tried to kill me an' tried to kill Angie…He deserved what he got on Parker's gibbet."

"Blood is blood." There was a muted pop and a hole appeared in the side of his Homberg.

Jack staggered backward and collapsed to his knees as both Fiona and Bill fired almost at the same time. Two rounds impacted Baldwin's chest, with the third creating a small hole between his eyes.

The man stood for a brief two seconds as a trickle of blood ran down the side of his nose, before he collapsed to the ground like a wet paper sack.

Baldwin's hat fell from his hands and tumbled several feet away, landing on its top. Inside, affixed to the crown, was a small twin-barreled .40 caliber derringer.

"Jack, Jack," Fiona screamed and ran to him.

He was curled up in a fetal position, squirming, moaning, and trying to breathe. Bill stepped over and eased Jack to his back. The position seemed to help as McGann took a deep breath and groaned.

"Oh, damn, what's Angie goin' to say," he finally gasped as he held both hands over his chest on the left side.

"There's no blood," said Bill as he searched Jack's chest and stomach area—finally moving his hands. "Hello...What's this?"

He unpinned Jack's Deputy United States Marshal's badge from his vest. "Well, what do you know?"

Bill held up the badge for Jack to see as he was still trying to catch his breath. Almost dead center, over the US in the middle of the star, was a deep dent. Roberts looked around at the ground and picked up a gray misshapened chunk of lead.

"Well, it's a good thing your badge isn't one of those cheap tin ones...looks like it's made from a Morgan silver dollar like mine. Stopped that bullet cold."

Jack continued to try to take deeper breaths and nodded in pain. "I wouldn't say cold. Think it busted a rib er two." He groaned as he rolled over and got to his knees. "Bass give it to me. Had one made fer the both of us when we started marshalin' together."

Fiona unbuttoned his vest and shirt, pulling them away from the impact site to show a bruise almost the size of a baseball that was getting darker by the second. "Well, this beats the alternative, I'd say, Jack."

He moaned again. "Uh, huh...Least now my Angie won't be so pissed. Tol' me not to come back with 'ny more holes in me."

Bill picked up Baldwin's hat and showed it to McGann.

Jack looked inside. "Well, looky there, the snake had a hideout shooter in his hat...like another miscreant we arrested once, Ben Larson. He had one of them little shooters in his guitar. But, this is a first. Hidin' it in his hat...ain't never heard the like," said Jack.

Bill and Fiona helped Jack to his feet.

"Know one thang."

"What's that?" asked Fiona.

"Ain't gonna be no laughin' er coughing…an' damn shore no sneezin' fer a spell." He held his hand against his chest and groaned again.

"Look," said Bill as he pointed up the hill.

The four giant white wolves that had been watching them, turned, jumped down from the boulders and disappeared from sight, one at a time.

"And there's *Bánushah Kuukuh Náttih,*" added Fiona.

"The Blue Water Woman," whispered Bill reverently.

The Caddo maiden looked directly at the trio for a moment, and then moved gracefully up the hillside. She paused briefly, looked back again, and continued her journey.

"She wants us to follow," commented Fiona.

"Not sure I can," said Jack.

Bill took McGann's left arm and Fiona his right.

"We'll help you," he said.

Jack nodded, groaned a little as they followed the figure. "Everthin's fine, long as I don't breathe."

"I don't think you've got any broken ribs, Jack, they're just severely bruised," Fiona commented. "If he'd had a bigger gun, you might be singing a different tune."

"Or not singin' atall…Thank God fer small favors." He looked up the hillside at the maiden's path. "Damnation, looks like she's headin' fer Crazy Mary's…this is gonna be interestin'."

The Blue Water Woman looked back once more, and then disappeared into the small six-by-four foot entrance to Mary's cave in the side of the mountain.

"Oh, boy," said Jack as they moved up to the opening.

"Should we go in?" asked Bill.

"That's where she went," said Fiona as she led the way. Bill and Jack followed single file.

The cave widened substantially after they passed through the tiny opening.

"Goin' to git real dark, real soon," commented Jack.

"I see one of Mary's lanterns," said Bill as he stepped over to the side wall. He picked it up from the floor of the cave and shook it. "Got coal oil in it…anybody got a match?"

Jack reached into his vest and pulled out his Bull Durham bag. There were four Lucifers stuck inside the label next to the makings paper. He handed Brushy Bill one. "Don't waste it."

"Try not to," said Roberts as he struck it on the rough stag grips of his Colt.

The strike-anywhere match hissed, sputtered, and then flared into a bright yellow flame, permeating the air with its sulfurous odor.

BLUE WATER WOMAN

Fiona lifted the glass globe for him and he touched the flame to the wick that extended about a quarter of an inch above the slot. The coal oil-soaked webbed cotton caught and she lowered the globe back down.

The lantern cast a pale yellow glow against the cave walls and dirt floor—its light stopped at a bend in the tunnel ahead.

Bill held it up a little over his head. "Well, shall we?"

"Just as well. She has to be in here somewhere," said Jack.

"Unless she vanished like she did in my sweatlodge vision," added Fiona. "What's that up ahead?"

They had turned the corner and the cave widened into a type of grotto. A trickle of water ran down one wall and created a crystal clear pool with a couple of travertine columns along the side.

There was a form consisting of what appeared to be a pile of furs and rags against a two foot diameter speleothem structure. Bill held the lantern closer.

"Oh, my God," exclaimed Fiona.

"It's Mary...or was," said Jack.

"She's mummified...must have died right there, leaning against that formation," added Bill. "But, how? We saw her yesterday."

Fiona pursed her lips and shook her head. "She apparently died years ago...ten, maybe fifteen."

"But, who the hell did we talk to?" asked Jack.

Fiona looked at the remains, and then at Jack and Bill. "*Bánushah Kuukuh Náttih*...She was Crazy Mary all along...Remember *Anompoli Lawa* said that therianthropy could include wolves, bear, hawks, panther, eagles, and even other people?"

Bill nodded. "Yeah, she took Crazy Mary's image and personality after she died to keep people scared away from this area where the treasure was hidden."

MCGANN HOME

"We must bury Mary Louise Waters in accordance with our customs...She was Chickasaw, after all. I will sanctify her remains and our ladies will make a white beaded doeskin burial gown for her. She will be buried with respect...Considering her life, she deserves it. She will join her murdered husband and babies in the afterlife," said *Anompoli Lawa* after he had been told of the story.

"Where will she be buried?"

"As you know, Bodie, the Chickasaw belong to the Muskogean clan of indigenous Americans and have been mound builders, like their relatives the Atakapan Tejas Caddo, for several thousands of years. We have a secret burial mound site that no white person is allowed to see...She was a member of *Nashobi*, the clan of the Wolf of the Chickasaw Nation like Alex Sixkiller's brother Ben. Her tribal name was *Tohbi Opa Taloowa*."

"Which means?" asked Fiona.

"White Singing Owl."

"That's so pretty," said Ruth Ann.

"She was actually a very beautiful woman before..." Winchester was unable to continue. "Well, you know."

"I'm sure that was part of the reason the Blue Water Woman chose her," said Fiona.

"I think we should seal that crevice in the cliff that leads to the treasure room."

"I agree, Jack. I believe that's what she wants," said Fiona.

TISHOMINGO
CHICKASAW NATION

Fiona, Jack, Angie and the others stood on the porch of a white frame house just outside of Tishomingo, the capital of the Chickasaw Nation. The women of the *Nashobi* clan inside had ceased the death chant.

Anompoli Lawa glanced toward the screen door. "It is time."

One of the Natives held the door open for four Chickasaw warriors in ceremonial white beaded doeskin war shirts. They reverently carried the burial pouch outside and laid it on a table under a large red oak tree. The tribal members gathered closely around the table with the others just behind them.

Anompoli Lawa, also dressed in a ceremonial fringed white doeskin shirt, pulled out a small beaded pouch from his medicine bag, which hung around his neck. He opened it, took a pinch of sacred dogwood pollen and scattered it to the four directions. He took another pinch and sprinkled it over the burial pouch and yet another straight up into the air to sanctify White Singing Owl's journey to the happy hunting grounds.

He took his personal totem of a Red-Tailed hawk from his medicine bag—it was carved from a piece of lightning-riven oak. With his right hand, he waved it above the remains and raising his other hand, he chanted in the Chickasaw tongue. *"Tohbi Opa Taloowa, Ababinili hoyo aboha ona. Chi-hóo-wah bya-chee…*May the Great Spirit guide you, White Singing Owl, that you may achieve your rest…Go with God."

The other tribal members repeated, *"Chi-hóo-wah bya-chee, Tohbi Opa Taloowa."*

Anompoli Lawa stepped back as the women of the tribe moved forward and began to softly sing a hymn—in the Chickasaw tongue.

Fiona nudged Bill and whispered, "Oh, my goodness, that's *Amazing Grace*, I recognize the melody...but it's in their language...It's unbelievably beautiful."

Anompoli Lawa overheard her comment and leaned closer. "We have sung that song for strength and at all burial ceremonies since our people were marched over the *Nunna daul Tsuny*...or the trail where we cried back in 1837."

§§§

EPILOGUE

RED RIVER BOTTOM

The full moon was rising over the tree line to the east in the gloaming as *Anompoli Lawa* replaced the skull in the mound in its proper location. Then he carefully laid the necklace below the skull and the pouches of pearls on each side. "Hand me the beaded doeskin, Fiona."

She removed a pale blue doeskin with very ornate and complicated beadwork from the Shaman's pouch and handed it to him.

"Our people came as close as they could to the artistic beadwork of our ancestors," he said, as he reverently covered the remains.

"Look," said Fiona.

Anompoli Lawa, Bill, Jim, Walt and Bodie glanced up to see four giant white wolves quietly stalking through the woods toward the clearing. All but Fiona and the Shaman drew their weapons and turned to face the perceived threat. Each wolf was at a different point, effectively encircling the clearing.

Anompoli Lawa ignored the lycanthropes as he removed the stopper from one of the canteens they brought from Arkansas and sprinkled the water over the doeskin and all around it. "With this sacred water I bless and sanctify this holy place. May the Blue Water Woman always sleep in tranquility and peace. *Yukit o-ita, Chí-hóo-wah-bya-chi a hoket tal.* May the Great Spirit walk with you, our holy mother."

The four wolves entered the clearing from different directions.

"Got company," Walt said as he cocked the hammer on his Colt.

The four men started backing in a circle toward *Anompoli Lawa* and Fiona at the mound.

A blue vapor issued in a writhing tendril from the mound and formed into a figure—the Blue Water Woman.

She turned to face the wolves and raised her hands. "Hold, my children. Be at peace. We are among friends." She turned to *Anompoli Lawa*. "I sense you are also a great Shaman."

Ken Farmer

He bowed his head in deference. "Not so great as *Bánushah Kuukuh Náttih*...Blue Water Woman. Your words flatter and humble me."

Walt and the others lowered their weapons.

"*Anompoli Lawa*, you have shown a spiritual kindness, great wisdom and understanding in the re-sanctifying of my resting place."

"The Blue Water Woman is well known as the Matron Saint of our cousins, the Atakapan Tejas Caddo Indians. She worked many miracles for her people through the wonderful blue nun, Sister Mary of Jesus of Ágreda...The Shamaness is a great protector and benefactor to many. I have always respected the beliefs and totems of my brothers and sisters," he answered.

She looked directly at Fiona. "And I sense in you, Fiona, the same goodness possessed by your ancestor and my mentor, Sister Mary of Jesus. You have a wonderful heart. I shall call you, *Báwsa' Hakáayu' Niish Iwi'*. In your language it means, See White Moon Eagle."

"Thank you, great *Bánushah Kuukuh Náttih*. I am honored." She bowed her head.

The Blue Water Woman looked back at *Anompoli Lawa*. "Now that you have re-sanctified this holy place, I can continue protecting my people that are left...Thank you for what you did up in the mountains for *Tohbi Opa Taloowa* and closing all

242

access to the vile Spanish treasure and bringing the evil ones to justice."

She bent over in front of the Chickasaw Shaman—who had been standing next to the mound supported by crutches with his foot in a cast—and passed her hands over his lower leg and foot, and then straightened up. "You are better now, *Anompoli Lawa*...put down your supports."

He dropped the crutches and leaned on his foot...it bore his weight. "There is no pain."

Bánushah Kuukuh Náttih smiled softly and nodded. "It shall be so."

"Great Blue Water Woman, with your permission, we will see that this sacred place is protected from desecration for all time," said Fiona.

The Shamaness raised her hands over her head. "I shall always be your personal totem, See White Moon Eagle."

She turned to the four giant wolves. "You may return to your original forms, my children."

The wolves changed into the four Native Americans Fiona and *Anompoli Lawa* had seen in their sweatlodge vision. There were two males and two females. The women were attired in buckskin dresses and the men in breechclouts.

The four knelt at the feet of the Blue Water Woman. She touched each one softly on the crown of their bowed heads. They rose to their feet, turned and vanished into the woods.

"I must also go now. My people will always be in your debt. *Chí-hóo-wah-bya-chi*...May the Great Spirit walk with you," she said in her liquid silk-like voice.

"*Chí-hóo-wah-bya-chia hoket tal*...Go with God, great spirit lady of the water," replied *Anompoli Lawa*.

The blue figure dissolved back into the light blue vapor and was drawn into the burial mound.

Fiona looked at the Shaman. "What did she mean, she would always be my personal totem?"

"You may think of it as she'll always be your Guardian Angel." *Anompoli Lawa* turned to the others. "You all know this never happened."

"What never happened?" asked Bodie.

"That's my godson," said Jack as he shook his head.

"No, really, I mean, what part of this never happened?"

Fiona put her hand on his shoulder. "Any of it, Bodie...Any of it."

SKEANS BOARDING HOUSE

"So, what happened while ya'll were up at the river?" asked Annabel.

Bodie glanced at Doctor Ashalatubbi, and then answered, "Oh, not much, Honey. The Doc blessed the artifacts with that water from up in Arkansas an' we reburied 'em...We drug as much deadfall and brush as we could find and covered the whole thing up so's you couldn't tell what it was...And I reckon that's about it."

"What about your foot, Winchester?" asked Faye. "I know it was broken and that bullet went all the way through."

He chuckled. "It must have been Angie's turpentine and tallow salve she packed it with while we were up in the Arbuckles...I've told you that stuff works miracles. You saw what it did for the wound in Bodie's chest."

Faye cocked a single eyebrow at the Chickasaw physician.

Walt spoke up, "Since Jack didn't need that steel-dust Saddlebred stallion of Baldwin's, he gave him to my daddy-in-law, Tom. My sweet Fran already has dibs on him soon as she's up and around after deliverin' our youngun...Oh, an' got some other good news...Marshal Lindsey found out from that feller Wheeler he captured up at the McGann's, what worked fer Baldwin...where the stole Bar M cattle was. The owner, Russ Marker, tells me he believes he's a gonna make it now that he's got his breedin' stock back."

Walt chuckled. "Says it was a funny thing, but them yahoos who was tryin' to buy his place have left town...Cain't find hide, hair er tallow of 'em."

"Uh, huh, funny how that works," said Fiona.

"Have you heard when they're going to have the special election for a new mayor and who's running?" asked Faye.

"The town council set it fer sixty days...and I'm pushin' Marshal Farmer to run...Don't know if that leg of his is ever goin' to be right. He don't need to be a roustin' drunk ne'er-do-wells out of the saloons," said Walt.

"I'd vote for him. There's one man that won't put up with any foolishness from the local politicians," offered Faye, and then she remembered something. "Oh, Fiona, a post came for you while ya'll were up at the river."

"Oh?"

She opened the lid to the small half-table next to the fireplace, removed a letter and handed it to Fiona, who was sitting on the dark green velvet settee.

Fiona looked at the white envelope. "It's from the president. Wonder what I did now?"

"Well, are you going to open it or just have it bronzed?" quipped Bill.

She cut her steel-gray eyes at him as she broke the wax presidential seal on the flap and removed the official-looking paper. "Don't push it, Marshal Roberts."

Fiona perused the letter, shook her head and got a wry grin on her face.

"Well?" asked Faye.

BLUE WATER WOMAN

She looked around at everyone in the parlor, and then cleared her throat. "'My dear Fiona, I have your letter of resignation from the United States Marshals Service on my desk. I take pen in hand to personally inform you of my outright and unequivocal rejection of same, and that I fully intend to tear it up, put it in my ashtray with my cigar stubs and burn it.

You, my dear, are far too valuable to the Marshals Service to lose. I am increasing your salary by ten percent and you shall report only to me, thereby saving you from the vicissitudes of going through the God-awful political merry-go-round here in Washington. Oh, for the days when everyone adhered to the Constitution—forgive me for my personal thoughts on the current state of politics in our country.

I am considering this matter closed and look forward to hearing of your future episodes, and thank Marshal Roberts for me for his recent telegram. I Remain Respectfully, Grover Cleveland - President'...Oh my goodness." She brought her hand to her mouth.

Fiona's eyes snapped at Brushy Bill. "Telegram? Future episodes? You have some explaining to do, Marshal Roberts."

Bill blushed, got a half grin on his face and stared at the floor. "I know."

§§§§

PREVIEW

THE NEXT EXCITING ADVENTURE

IN THE

LADY LAW SAGA

FLYNN

by

KEN FARMER

FLYNN

CROSS, TEXAS

"Hands in the air, pilgrims. We're makin' a withdrawal today. Don't do anything stupid…and by the way, I'm not in the habit of repeatin' myself," said the stocky, broad-shouldered man, politely, from behind a blue calico bandana. He held a sawed-off double-barreled shotgun at his waist. "This here scattergun can make quite a mess."

The customers of the Cattlemen's Bank of Cross, three men and one woman, threw their hands up as one. The other three bandits divided up the duties. Two handed small flour sacks to the cashiers to be filled, while the third passed his bag around to the customers, relieving them of their valuables.

"Git a move on, boys. Don't have all day," said the leader as he walked over to the mahogany door that had Finus T. Merkins - President, printed in gold lettering on the upper half.

He tapped on the door with his knuckles. "Excuse me sir, could you step out here for a moment. I'd like to make a sizable withdrawal."

A portly man with thick white mutton-chop whiskers, in an expensive three-piece suit, opened the door to find himself staring down the barrels of the robber's shot gun.

"What's all this then?" he blustered.

"Like I said, I'd like to make a sizable withdrawal…say everything you have in your safe…if you please."

"What? What? Why, this is an outrage. You ruffians get out of my bank."

The robber poked Merkins forcibly in his ample paunch with the shotgun. "That makes me angry there, Finus, and you don't want to do that…I said please."

"I don't give a jot or a tittle what you said, I want you and these men…say, I know you! Your name's…"

Finus T. Merkins didn't get to say anything else as the man behind the mask pulled both triggers on the twelve gauge and sent all twenty-four double ought buckshot into him at close range. Blood and intestines covered everything within five feet, including the outlaw.

"Damn you, that really makes me mad…I told you." He looked down at his blood and gut spattered dark broadcloth suit, and then up to his men. "You know what to do."

He turned and headed for the nine foot double front doors and burst through them to the boardwalk outside. The fifth man in the gang, Goose Garson, was minding the horses.

"What happened, boss?" he asked.

"What do you think? Stupid-assed banker thought he recognized me. Hold this." He pitched Goose his shotgun and stepped over to the horse trough, pulled off his kerchief and tried to clean as much of the gore from his face and clothes as he could.

Five rapid shots followed by a single one rang out from inside the bank, and then his three other men stepped outside with their bags of loot, looked up and down the street of the small rural town for heroes and moved to their horses.

Townspeople were peeking out from alleyways and storefronts, wisely trying not to be seen.

The well-built, mustachioed leader rinsed his kerchief one final time, tied it around his neck and swung into the saddle of his claybank gelding. "Let's ride, boys."

SHERIFF'S OFFICE
JACKSBORO, TEXAS

"Sheriff! Sheriff...The bank's been robbed...Got a telegram from the town marshal."

"Whoa, hold on there Deputy Platt, slow down...Where and when?" asked Sheriff Flynn.

"Oh, right...Over to Cross an' jest now. Got the telegram jest now," said the nineteen-year old sandy-haired deputy as he waved the yellow slip of paper in the air.

The square-jawed, middle-aged, broad-shouldered sheriff shook his head. "No...*When* was the bank robbed?"

The deputy looked at the flimsy. "Uh...'bout thirty minutes ago, looks like...sir."

Flynn snapped his fingers twice at Platt.

"Oh, yessir." The young deputy handed him the telegram.

The sheriff's sky-blue eyes perused the missive, and then looked back up. "Go round up some of the boys for a posse...seven or eight oughta do. I'm goin' down to the livery and get my horse...Have everybody meet out front here in ten minutes. Got it?"

"Yessir." Platt turned on his heel and headed to the door.

"Get your scattergun, son."

The young deputy spun about, quickly stepped over to the gun rack and grabbed a Remington pump-action 12-gauge. "Got it, sir."

Once again he headed to the door.

"Shells, Platt. You need shells."

"Oh, right, sir." He ducked his head in embarrassment and opened the drawer beneath the rack. "Uh, single or double ought, sir?"

Flynn looked at him from under the brim of his gray Stetson with the gold and black acorn cord and crossed sabers he'd worn since his cavalry days. "Doesn't really matter much, Deputy, now does it?"

"Yessir, uh, no sir." He grabbed a box of single ought and dumped the contents in his coat pocket.

"Go ahead and load it now. Gun's not much good not loaded...is it?"

"Uh, no, sir." Platt thumbed five shells into the tubular magazine and slipped the sling over his left shoulder.

Flynn nodded at him. "Now, you want to go round up that posse?...Sometime today?"

"Yessir."

He grabbed the knob, pulled the door inward and hit his foot. The door bounced back and slammed shut. Platt glanced at the sheriff, stepped back a little and eased the door open. He quickly darted through, only to hang the shotgun sling on the doorknob, jerking him backward to his butt on the boardwalk and slamming the door closed behind him.

Sheriff Flynn shook his head, looked up and grinned. "God help him…or better yet, help me."

A little over ten minutes later, seven mounted townsmen plus Platt, joined Sheriff Flynn in front of the office.

"All right, people, you know the routine. Stay behind me and don't do anything I don't tell you, understand?…Just nod."

They all nodded.

"We'll head in the direction of Bryson. Should cut their sign somewhere between here and there…Let's ride."

The former cavalry officer nudged his blue roan Morgan gelding up into a road trot and led the posse out of town to the southwest.

Three miles from Jacksboro and five miles south of Cross, Flynn bumped his horse back to a walk, and then to a halt. "Whoa, Laddie."

He studied the ground for a moment, looked over his right shoulder to the north, and then to the south.

"That them, Sheriff?" asked Gerald Haney, the owner of Haney's Livery.

"My guess…There's five of 'em and they're at an extended trot…Headed in the direction of Grayford."

"Ain't that in Palo Pinto County?" inquired Buck Whitehead, the town smithy.

"It is."

"Purty rough country," said Haney.

"That too." Flynn reined Laddie to the left and squeezed him into a mile-eating rocking chair lope. The others followed suit.

The posse had broken back down to an extended trot as they approached a rocky ridge to the south. The narrow rutted wagon road was bordered on either side by post oak and mesquite. There was an open area over two hundred yards wide between the end of the tree-shrouded road to the rocks up ahead.

The sheriff held up his hand, the posse slowed to a walk and finally stopped at the edge of the tree line.

"What's the matter, Sheriff? Lose the tracks?"

Flynn frowned at the young deputy. "Not hardly…Ya'll see that ridge up yonder?"

They nodded.

"Prime place for an ambush if any of 'em are watchin' their back trail."

Ken Farmer

A limb right beside Platt's head snapped off with a click, followed a half-second later by the boom of a rifle.

"Jesus all mighty," the deputy said as he ducked and backed his horse into the cover of the trees.

"We better take cover 'fore that shooter gits the range."

"He already has the range, Haney...He hit exactly what he was aimin' at." Flynn spotted the cloud of gunsmoke halfway up the ridge and frowned. "That hogback is in Palo Pinto County...Out of my jurisdiction anyway. Let's head back."

SKEANS BOARDING HOUSE

"Oh, damn," said Fiona Miller, as she finished reading a telegram.

"What?" asked Marshal Brushy Bill Roberts as he looked up from reading the latest edition of the Gainesville Daily Register.

"Another bank robbery...in Cross, just west of Jacksboro."

"That makes four in the last two weeks."

She nodded. "They're calling him the gentleman bandit, because he's usually very polite and doesn't hurt anyone...This time though, they killed everyone in the bank, including one woman."

"Damnation...Who sent the telegram?"

"Sheriff Mason Flynn, in Jacksboro. He said he tracked the robbers until they left his jurisdiction and crossed into Palo Pinto County…."

"Isn't that where Oliver Loving and Charlie Goodnight are from?"

"It is…Loving died in '67."

"Yeah, read about it. He died at Fort Sumner, New Mexico, of gangrene…after a run-in with some Comanches on a cattle drive. Oliver had told Charlie he wanted to be buried at Weatherford…Goodnight brought his body all the way back from Fort Sumner. He and Goodnight were in partnership in the cattle business with John Chisum in the Bosque Grande…just south of there…That was some time before I came to that part of the country."

Bill picked up his coffee cup and took a sip. "Mister Chisum's sister, Nancy, is married to Loving's cousin, B.F. Bourland. I met her and her husband when I worked for John in '78."

"Goodnight still has a ranching operation in Palo Pinto County, as well as up in the panhandle, the JA Ranch in the Palo Duro Canyon."

"The Goodnight-Loving Trail…now, that's some real history. Charlie invented the chuck wagon, you know?…To feed the cowhands on trail drives."

"It's a small world...What with Chisum moving to Lincoln County from here in Cooke County back in '66 and you working for him in your younger days."

"In a roundabout way, all that business back in Lincoln County is how I finally became a Deputy US Marshal."

Fiona cocked her head. Her long raven hair was draped loosely over her left shoulder. "How so?"

"I became friends with a Deputy US Marshal, Robert A. Widenmann...he got me out of jail once there and advised me that I'd live a longer life if I moved to the back side of the chase."

"Other than being on the scout and running from the law?"

He grinned and nodded. "So to speak."

"I'd say that proved to be sage advice...Marshal Roberts. Well, what do you say we go downtown and send a telegram to Sheriff Flynn that we'll be there in two days...We'll have to ride the boys since there're no trains going through that area as yet."

"Sounds good, Marshal Miller. I'll treat you to lunch at the Fried Pie after we send the telegram."

"Sounds like an offer I can't refuse."

"Did I hear you say you're buyin' lunch?" asked Bodie Hickman from the foyer as he came in the front door.

FLYNN

Bill glanced over at the young Texas Ranger as he hung his hat on the hall tree. "Well that was a fortuitous entry...Where've you been?"

"Down to Walt's office, helpin' him orientate the new deputies on the laws an' such...an' how to make arrests without gittin' yerself kilt."

Fiona noticed the top of a yellow envelope sticking out of his coat pocket. "Get a telegram?"

Bodie pulled the filmsey out and handed it to her. "Oh, yeah. From my captain down to Austin. Seems there's been a rash of bank robberies over in Jack, Clay, Parker and Wise counties...Want me to ride over and shut it down."

Bill and Fiona exchanged glances.

"Well, we should just as well ride over together. Sheriff Flynn at Jacksboro has asked for our help, too," said Fiona.

"When do we leave?" asked Bodie.

"First thing in the morning," said Fiona.

THE FRIED PIE
GAINESVILLE, TEXAS

"The lunch special today is, pan-fried steak, fresh field peas, buttered corn and creamed new potatoes, along with a basket

259

of hot yeast rolls, of course," said the waitress, Maybel Newsom, to Fiona, Bill and Bodie.

"What are ya'll havin' to drink?" the full-figured woman asked.

The two men looked at Fiona to go first.

"Iced sweet tea for me," she said. "With a sprig of mint, if you don't mind."

"Buttermilk, please and thank you," said Bodie.

"Sweet tea for me too, Maybel," added Bill as he got to his feet, walked over to the newspaper rack, got a copy of yesterday's Dallas Morning News and headed back to his chair.

He unfolded the paper and scanned the front page headlines. After a moment of perusing the news of the world, and then the local, Bill looked up. "Well, well, this is interesting."

He glanced at their waitress as she set their drinks on the table.

"Be right back with your plates," Maybel said.

"What's that?" asked Fiona.

"Says here a space craft crashed near Aurora a couple of days ago."

"What's a space craft?" asked Bodie.

Bill looked over at the ranger. "Did you ever read *From the Earth to the Moon* by Jules Verne?"

"Well, actually, I did…He wrote it in '65, I believe. Had to baby sit several shipments of gold coin from Denver to Dallas by train, couple years ago. Had a lot of time to read on the trips."

"Well, that projectile they shot out of what Verne called a Columbiad space gun toward the moon was a 'space craft'."

"What the Sam Hill would a space craft projectile be doin' crashin' near Aurora?"

"Where's Aurora?" asked Fiona.

Bill glanced her way. "In Wise County, northwest of Fort Worth and east of Boyd…about fifty miles southwest of Gainesville."

"I thought that book was just fiction," said Fiona.

"Well, listen to this from yesterday's paper." Bill started to read, "'Dallas Morning News, April 19, 1897'…the by-line is a fellow named E.E. Haydon…'Space Craft Crashes Near Aurora, Texas…Pilot Killed…'"

"You mean somebody was in that thing?" exclaimed Bodie.

Bill nodded. "That's what the paper says." He continued to read aloud, "'Aurora, Wise County, Texas, April 17, 1897…About 6 o'clock this morning the early risers of Aurora were astonished at the sudden appearance of the airship which has been sailing around the country. It was traveling due north and much nearer the earth than before. Evidently some of the

261

machinery was out of order, for it was making a speed of only ten or twelve miles an hour, and gradually settling toward the earth. It sailed over the public square and when it reached the north part of town it collided with the tower of Judge Proctor's windmill and went into pieces with a terrific explosion, scattering debris over several acres of ground, wrecking the windmill and water tank and destroying the judge's flower garden. The pilot of the ship is supposed to have been the only one aboard and, while his remains were badly disfigured, enough of the original has been picked up to show that he was not an inhabitant of this world.'...Son of a Gun." He looked over at Bodie and Fiona.

Maybel walked up to the table and set their steaming plates in front of them. "Will there be anything else I can git ya'll?"

"This should be fine, thank you," said Fiona.

Bill picked up with the story where he left off, "...'Mr. T.J. Weems, the U.S. Army Signal Service officer at this place and an authority on astronomy, gives it as his opinion that the pilot was a native of the planet Mars.'"

"Excuse me?" Bodie said.

Roberts arched his eyebrows and shrugged his shoulders. "'Papers found on his person—evidently the records of his travels—are written in some unknown hieroglyphics and cannot be deciphered. This ship was too badly wrecked to form any conclusion as to its construction or motive power. It was built of an unknown metal, resembling somewhat a mixture of aluminum and silver, and it must have weighed several tons. The town is today full of people who are viewing the wreckage and gathering specimens of strange metal from the debris. The pilot's funeral will take place tomorrow'."

"'There are more things in heaven and earth, Horatio, than are dreamt of in your philosophy'," Fiona mused when he had finished reading the article.

"An apt quote from Hamlet, m'lady," said Bill.

"Holy cow, that's really interestin'…Ya'll actually think there could be other people out there?" Bodie pointed up.

Fiona had cut a piece of her pan steak and was chewing the tasty breaded morsel when Hickman looked at her after asking his question.

She swallowed, and then answered, "I think it would be the height of egotism and folly to think that we are the only form of life in the wide universe…You know that each of the thousands upon thousands of stars we see in our night sky is a sun just like ours…"

"And to think that each one could have one or more worlds goin' around it like this one here?" Bodie shook his head and scooped up a forkful of peas.

Fiona nodded at him. "We know from our recent experience with the Blue Water Woman and Anna that shapeshifting and spirits actually do exist…Who are we to say that there aren't other intelligent creatures out there…maybe not like us or…maybe they are. Who knows?"

"In the South Asia Indian Mahabharata and Ramayana writings, there are descriptions of what they called Vimanas or flying machines," said Bill.

"That's true. Even in this day and age, we don't have anything that can fly, except for balloons…and whatever crashed into that Judge Proctor's windmill, was apparently no balloon," added Fiona as she buttered a fresh roll.

"Too bad Doctor Ashalatubbi isn't here. I'll bet he knows some stories the ancient Indians of America tell about aliens…or sky gods, as they called them," said Bill.

"Ya'll're makin' my head hurt," said Bodie as he cut a big piece of his steak and popped it in his mouth with his fork.

"We'll have to come back by way of Aurora and look around after we take care of things in Jacksboro," said Bill. "It's only about thirty miles from there."

Maybel walked up after they had finished their lunches. "Would ya'll like a fried pie for desert?"

"I would indeed, Madam…I'd like a fried buttermilk," said Bill.

"Fried buttermilk pie? There ain't no such of a thing. You cain't make a fried buttermilk pie," exclaimed Bodie.

"Are you willing to bet on that, Ranger?" challenged Fiona.

He looked first at Fiona, then at Bill, and then up at Maybel who was just standing there with her head cocked and grinning.

"Don't guess I got a choice, do I?"

"I wouldn't think so," said Bill.

"Three buttermilk fried pies, if you please," said Fiona.

"Coming right up." Maybel turned and headed toward the kitchen.

In less than five minutes, she set small plates in front of everyone. In the center of each was a half-moon steaming hot fried pie right out of the skillet with a dollop of fresh melting butter on the top—the edges of the crust had been finger crimped.

Maybel placed a clean fork beside each plate and grinned like a possum eating persimmons. "Enjoy," she said as she folded her arms over her ample bosom.

Bodie looked at each of his friends again, picked up his fork, spread the melted butter around and cut the end from the flaky brown southern delicacy. He glanced at the firm, ivory-colored, creamy filling, and then stuck it in his mouth.

"Oh...my...God...I have died and gone to heaven," he said after he swallowed. "Never in my longest days would I have figured you could put buttermilk pie inside one of these fried crusts…Never."

He looked up at Maybel still standing by the table with her arms crossed over her chest. "Fact is, I may jest have to have another, Ma'am."

"Don't let your eyes get bigger than your stomach, Bodie…they're pretty rich," said Fiona.

A big grin spread across his face. "Believe I can handle it." He lifted another large piece to his mouth, closed his eyes and slowly savored the buttery flavored confectionery before he swallowed it with orgasmic pleasure.

WISE COUNTY, TEXAS

A small—only four-foot-ten—young looking girl with big expressive brown eyes, peeked at the farm house near Boyd, from under a juniper tree. She watched as the middle-aged woman of the house finished hanging wet-wash on the clothesline at the side of a white dog-run style house with a wrap-around front porch.

A few moments after the woman went back inside, the little girl rubbed the bracelet on her left wrist, crawled out from under the tree, ran to the clothesline, jerked a small green print calico dress free and darted back to the clump of cedars.

She crawled deeper into the copse of trees and pulled the still damp homemade cotton dress over her head, only slightly messing her light brown pixie hairstyle.

The child touched the bracelet again, picked up an old carpet bag she had found in a storage shed for her belongings. She stole away out the backside of the junipers and worked her way into some woods that ran along both sides of a small waterway known locally as Deep Creek. It joined the West Fork of the Trinity River which flowed past Jacksboro to the west before reaching the small farming community of Boyd.

§§

TIMBER CREEK PRESS

BLACK STAR BAY by T.C. Miller
BLACKSTAR MOUNTAIN by T.C. Miller

HISTORICAL FICTION WESTERN
THE NATIONS by Ken Farmer and Buck Stienke
HAUNTED FALLS by Ken Farmer and Buck Stienke
HELL HOLE by Ken Farmer
ACROSS the RED by Ken Farmer and Buck Stienke
BASS and the LADY by Ken Farmer and Buck Stienke
DEVIL'S CANYON by Buck Stienke
LADY LAW by Ken Farmer

SY/FY
LEGEND of AURORA by Ken Farmer & Buck Stienke
AURORA: INVASION by Ken Farmer & Buck Stienke

HISTORICAL FICTION ROMANCE
THE TEMPLAR TRILOGY
MYSTERIOUS TEMPLAR by Adriana Girolami
THE CRIMSON AMULET by Adriana Girolami

Coming Soon

HISTORICAL FICTION WESTERN
FLYNN by Ken Farmer

HISTORICAL FICTION ROMANCE
TEMPLAR'S REDEMPTION by Adriana Girolami

MILITARY ACTION/TECHNO
BLACKSTAR RANCH by T.C. Miller

SY/FY
ANTAREAN DILEMMA by T.C. Miller